Praise for
AMY PATRICIA MEADE

"Amy Patricia Meade is a real find!" —*Mystery Scene*

"Sprightly characters, saucy dialog, and supple pacing are once again winsomely showcased in Meade's sassy paean to those zany Depression-era, romantic detective duos."—*Booklist* (for Meade's *Shadow Waltz*)

"A smart little drawing-room mystery that will delight fans of Golden Age murder."—*Toronto Globe and Mail* (for Meade's *Black Moonlight*)

"With great aplomb, Marjorie ferrets out the truth in a traditional whodunit that boasts nary a dull moment." —*Publishers Weekly* (for Meade's *Black Moonlight*)

"Full of tongue-in-cheek humor and witty dialog, this entertaining puzzle will appeal to fans of Carolyn Hart and Agatha Christie."—*Library Journal* (for Meade's *Black Moonlight*)

Chelsea R. Nye

About the Author

AMY PATRICIA MEADE, the author of the critically acclaimed Marjorie McClelland Mysteries, is a native of Long Island, NY, where she earned bachelor's degrees in English and business. She enjoys traveling, cooking, and classic films, and is a member of Sisters in Crime and Mystery Writers of America. Her Pret' Near Perfect Mystery series debuts this November with *Well-Offed in Vermont*, and she is the author of the forthcoming Rosie the Riveter Mystery series (Kensington). Meade now lives in Vermont and spends the long New England winters writing mysteries with a humorous or historical bent.

Visit Amy on the Internet at www.amypatriciameade.com.

AMY PATRICIA MEADE

Well-Offed
IN
VERMONT

A PRET' NEAR PERFECT
MYSTERY

MIDNIGHT INK
WOODBURY, MINNESOTA

First Edition
Second Printing, 2011

Book design and edit by Rebecca Zins
Cover design by Ellen Lawson
Cover illustration ©Tim Zeltner/i2i Art Inc.
Interior needle and thread image ©2004 Nova Development/Art Explosion

Midnight Ink, an imprint of Llewellyn Worldwide Ltd.

Library of Congress Cataloging-in-Publication Data
Meade, Amy Patricia, 1972–
Well-offed in Vermont: a pret' near perfect mystery / Amy Patricia Meade.—
   1st ed.
   p.   cm.
ISBN 978-0-7387-2590-1
1. Married people—Fiction. 2. Murder—Investigation—Fiction.
3. Vermont—Fiction. I. Title.
PS3613.E128W45 2011
813'.6—dc22

                                                           2011020453

Midnight Ink
Llewellyn Worldwide Ltd.
2143 Wooddale Drive
Woodbury, MN 55125-2989

www.midnightinkbooks.com

Printed in the United States of America

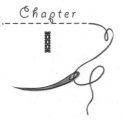

Chapter
1

STELLA THORNTON BUCKLEY carefully navigated her bright yellow 2008 Smart Fortwo coupe up the quarter-mile-long potholed dirt driveway and watched with a mix of trepidation and excitement as each revolution of the vehicle's fifteen-inch tires brought her closer to the circa 1890 white clapboard farmhouse ahead.

White-knuckled, Stella gripped the steering wheel and cringed as she felt her stomach churn and her heart rate rise with each teeth-rattling bump and dip. She didn't recall the driveway being in such bad repair during their last visit, but it was certainly something that she and Nick would need to address. "Let the homeowner's remorse begin," she said to herself as she brought the diminutive vehicle to a stop directly in front of the farmhouse's extensive wraparound porch, just a few yards behind the massive U-Haul moving truck operated by her husband.

Dressed in a New York Giants T-shirt and a pair of well-worn jeans, Graham Nicholas Buckley—Nick to all who knew him—stepped down from the driver's seat and, with a deep yawn, stretched his arms above his solid six-foot-two-inch-tall frame.

Stella, meanwhile, retrieved her cell phone from its place on the passenger seat and stared blankly at the last-received-call display. Home repairs were the least of her concerns. As if the drive from New York City and the subsequent house closing hadn't been tiring enough, the call she had received while on the road had left her feeling completely depleted. The Shelburne Museum, home to one of the nation's most diverse collections of Americana, had given their textiles curator position—the only available job of its type within the state of Vermont—to another applicant.

Fighting back tears, Stella switched off the phone and watched through the front windshield as Nick, sporting a boyish grin, sprinted to the front of the U-Haul. She had mentioned nothing to him about the Shelburne call. This move, the farmhouse, the Forest Service job that was to start the following Monday—all of it—had been Nick's dream for as long as she'd known him. That dream was finally coming true, and Stella was determined not to allow her personal disappointment to mar the occasion.

Her resolve strengthened, she withdrew the keys from the Smart car's ignition. Upon snatching her sweatshirt from the back of the driver's seat, she leapt from behind the wheel and rushed to the front of the truck where Nick now stood, arms folded across his chest, surveying the structure before him.

"I can't believe we did it," he remarked in amazement. "I can't believe we're here."

"Not only are we here," she dangled a single gold key in front of her husband's face, "but we're here to stay."

Nick grabbed the key in one hand and placed the other on the small of Stella's back. "Homeowners," he said, meditatively turning the key over in the palm of his hand.

"Vermont homeowners," she amended.

Nick turned his gaze to the seemingly endless forest of brightly colored trees that surrounded the back of the farmhouse. Beyond them, the rounded gray peaks of the Green Mountains, like a row of balding elder statesmen, stood sentinel over the valley below. "Helluva better view than the one on Murray Hill, isn't it?"

"Oh, I don't know. When Mr. Yang got his annual shipment of chrysanthemums in, that corner market was just as colorful." The early October air had grown damp and chilly, prompting Stella to don her hooded sweatshirt and pull the zipper up tightly against her chin. "Perhaps not as picturesque as this, mind you, but—"

Nick pulled his wife closer and laughed. "Yeah, you look like you're enjoying the scenery. Come on, let's get inside before it rains." He led her up the porch steps to the front door, which, after a bit of key-jiggling, unlocked and then swung wide open.

Eager to escape the bone-chilling wind, Stella stepped toward the doorsill, only to feel Nick's strong arms lift her off the ground and playfully throw her over his shoulder. "Watch your head."

"What are you doing?" Stella ducked and giggled as he carried her across the threshold.

"It's tradition for a husband to carry his wife into their new home, isn't it?" He continued through the foyer, past the spindled staircase, and into the first room on the right.

"Yes, but typically not in a fireman carry. And not all the way into—" From her unique, upside-down vantage point, Stella could see that the living room—which had, upon last inspection, been empty—now bore a large air mattress piled high with blankets, a basket of firewood and matches, and, on the hearth, a bottle of champagne with two glasses. "What—? What's all this? How did you—?"

Nick put her down gently. "I called the real-estate office from the road and asked Alice to set it up."

"*That's* why she was late for closing."

"Uh-huh. I wanted it to be a surprise—as my way of saying thank you."

"It's a lovely surprise." Stella threw her arms around her husband's neck and embraced him tightly. "But why do you need to thank me?"

"For leaving New York. For moving here. For letting me pursue my career." Nick brushed his lips against her dark blond hair.

She took a step back and looked into his dark hazel eyes. "Hey, when we got married, we agreed that if, after five years, I still hadn't been promoted to curator, we'd move somewhere that would allow you to do fieldwork. That was the deal, right?"

"Yeah, but that was five years ago. Not many women would have stuck to it the way you did."

"I stuck to it because I love you," she said. "And because I know that working a government desk job wasn't what you had in mind when you got your degree in forestry. But you turned down a field position and put your career on hold so that I could continue on at the museum."

"And now you've put *your* career on hold for *me*."

It was tempting to disclose her recent failure, to tell her husband about the Shelburne job and then take solace in his sheltering arms. But Nick had waited five years for this day, and Stella was determined not to let anything ruin it. "What are you talking about? I haven't put anything on hold. I have a résumé in with the

Shelburne Museum, remember? I'm just waiting to hear if the job will come through."

"And if it doesn't?"

"There are plenty of historical sites around that might need a curator."

"Of medieval tapestries?" Nick raised a skeptical eyebrow.

"Of something," Stella shrugged. "Tapestries are my specialty, but I'm sure this area offers a whole realm of items that are just as interesting."

"Yeah, I heard maple sugar buckets are fascinating. And then, of course, there's the farm equipment and milking machines."

"Don't forget the antique cheese molds."

"Why would someone visit a museum of moldy cheese?" Nick deadpanned.

Stella rolled her eyes. "Whatever I decide to specialize in, rest assured that it will be something I enjoy."

"I hope so. The new field position pays better than my desk job, so you don't have to settle for a job you don't like."

"I know. I won't; I promise. Right now, however, we're celebrating you and your career and our new home … after we unload that truck, of course."

"No unloading the truck," Nick contradicted with a smile.

"What do you mean, no unloading the truck?"

"Just that: no unloading the truck. Not today, anyway. We only have a couple hours of daylight left and, if my outdoorsman instinct is correct, it's going to rain any second now."

Nick pointed to the set of twelve-over-twelve windows that punctuated the front of the living room window and paused, but the deluge he had predicted failed to materialize.

"Okay, maybe not any second," he revised with a grin. "Still, what you need—what we *both* need—is to relax. Between the going-away parties, packing, loading the truck, paperwork, the drive … it's been crazy."

"You're right. It has been a whirlwind."

"Mmm-hmm." Nick wrapped his arms around her waist and tilted his head toward hers. "What do you say I start the fire, pour us some champagne, and then later on, we can grab a bite at that bar and grill we passed on the way into town?"

"And in between the champagne and dinner?" she asked coyly, her gray-blue eyes sparkling in the dwindling late afternoon light.

"We'll see if we can't warm you up." Nick unzipped his wife's sweatshirt and left her with a lingering kiss before starting to work on the fire.

Stella, meanwhile, set about draping one of the large woven blankets over the front windows. As she worked to obstruct the view of potential visitors, large drops of water came crashing down onto the driveway and the front porch steps. "Hey, it's raining."

"See? I wasn't too far off. My senses are just dulled from all the city noise and pollution. Give me a few months of living here and I'll be able to predict rainstorms, snow accumulations, and the sex of unborn calves."

"That's fabulous," Stella replied dryly. "I'm sure your folks in New Jersey will be very proud."

Nick laughed and looked up from the pile of wood he had stacked, in crisscross fashion, inside the hearth. "What are you doing?"

"Covering the window."

"I can see that. Why?"

"For some privacy."

"Uh … you do realize the nearest house is over a half mile away, don't you?"

Stella tossed the last bit of blanket over the empty curtain rod and then stepped back to examine her work. "Yes, but this way, if someone drops by, they can't see us … *you know*."

"Who's going to drop by? No one knows we're here."

"Well … I don't know. I guess you can take the girl out of New York but you can't take the New York out of the girl." She sat on the edge of the air mattress and watched as Nick deftly lit the kindling. "But I, like you, will adjust. Yep, give me a few months and I'll be used to living in the middle of nowhere with dirt roads, no neighbors, and no blinds. In fact, I may even take to walking around the house naked."

"No complaints here," Nick replied as he stoked the fire with a long stick. "But your mother on Long Island will be horrified."

"You think maybe that will keep her from visiting?"

"Doubt it. If I were you, I'd say we moved to a small town where cigarettes, vermouth, and polyester stretch pants are outlawed. She'll never step foot near the place."

Stella pulled a face. "Eh … I'm not sure that's enough."

"Okay, tell her that all the elderly men in town lost their retirement funds in the banking crisis and now take turns working part-time shifts at the McDonald's in Rutland. If poverty doesn't keep your mother at bay, nothing else will."

Stella frowned, recalling the day her mother, Lila, filed for divorce from her father, Michael Thornton, citing irreconcilable differences. In truth, the only thing in their marriage that could not be reconciled was Michael's New York City police detective's paycheck with Lila's need to finance weekly hair appointments, shopping sprees, bridge clubs, cocktail parties, and the other female trappings of success she saw her society friends enjoying. But with custody a non-issue—Stella, their only child, was to start college that fall—Michael saw little reason to fight the divorce. Desolate, he agreed to Lila's demands and consequently wound up funding her gold-digging escapades for the next eighteen years, first through his alimony payments and then, more recently, through his widow's death benefit.

"And not a country club for miles. You know, honey, if we stick to that story, we may even be able to scare her into moving down to Boca."

"We should be that lucky." Satisfied with the fire he had produced, Nick grabbed the bottle of champagne from the ice bucket and started to remove the wire cage. "Now if we can only find a way to keep my parents from vacationing here—"

"I love your parents!" Stella interrupted.

"Of course you do. They worship the ground you walk on."

"No, they don't."

"Yes, they do. My mother is always calling to ask you for recipes and fashion advice."

"Who else is she going to call? She has two sons and only one daughter-in-law."

"And my dad? He thinks you're the greatest thing since La-Z-Boy started putting cup holders in their recliners."

"I don't know, he's awfully fond of those cup holders."

"They don't rate quite as high as you do, though."

"Oh, stop it," Stella laughed. "You know your parents love you."

"And I love them. But I don't want to have to remind myself of that every day of their four-week stay."

"Is that how long they stay with your brother?"

Nick nodded.

"Wow. Okay ... we'll just have to tell them that we don't have cable television and that pocketing Sweet'N Low from restaurants is a state offense."

"You know, you may be even more terrific than my parents claim." Nick wrapped the neck of the champagne bottle with the front of his shirt, revealing a smooth chest and stomach, both of which had been finely sculpted by hours of exercise and field training.

"You're, um, pretty terrific yourself."

Nick replied to the statement with a pop of the champagne cork. Once the initial spate of foam had subsided, he dispensed the bubbling, straw-colored beverage into the waiting glasses and passed a flute to Stella. "To you," he toasted and clinked the rim of his glass against hers.

"To us." She took a celebratory sip and felt her body warm as the citrusy effervescence of the champagne burst against her palate. "Mmm, very nice."

"Glad you like it. I asked Alice to pick it out, since, as you know, I'm"—Nick smacked his lips together and stuck his tongue out in an expression of distaste—"not a fan." He placed his glass on the hearth, rose to his feet, and disappeared down the hallway, only to return a few seconds later with a bottle of beer. "Fortunately, I also asked her to pick up six of these." He extracted a multifunction knife from his pocket and used it to pry off the cap before sitting back down.

"Domestic beer," Stella noted as she tilted her glass against the neck of the brown bottle. "To you and your budget-minded taste buds."

"New homeowners need to make sacrifices," he stated before taking another swig. "Besides, there are other ways of getting a buzz."

In the glow of the fire, Nick's eyes appeared deep brown instead of the green-laden tone they undertook in daylight. Stella was tempted to lean forward and bestow upon him a kiss that would overshadow all their previous kisses, but she decided instead to string him along just a bit longer.

"Oh yeah, I've heard about Vermont's reputation for illegal substances. But you know, honey, it's been nearly twenty years since you graduated college. Aren't you past that experimental age?"

"That's not exactly what I meant."

"Oh?" She sipped her champagne artlessly. "What did you have in mind?"

The half-empty beer bottle made a dull clunk as Nick set it down on the hardwood floor. Reaching his arms around Stella's narrow waist, he pulled her close to him and kissed her, nearly sending the contents of her glass spilling onto her sweatshirt.

"Ah, I give you a buzz, do I?" She set her champagne glass beside Nick's beer bottle.

"As if you need to ask. Now give me a kiss or I'll put you back in that fireman's carry and spank you."

"Promises, promises," she teased before complying with her husband's command.

Nick returned the kiss and then some. Removing her sweatshirt hungrily, he eased Stella back onto the air mattress and let his lips travel slowly from her mouth and to her chin, then down the length of her neck.

"I love you," she stated breathlessly.

He sat up, pulled his shirt over his head, and flung it on the floor. "I love you too," he whispered as he leaned in for another kiss.

Just then, there was the sound of a distant knock.

Stella hoisted herself up on her elbows. "What was that?"

"Probably just the house settling," Nick dismissed, his focus concentrated upon the task of seducing his wife.

She sat motionless and waited for the noise to repeat itself, all the while trying to ignore her husband's fingertips as they travelled beneath her fitted black T-shirt, circled her navel, and then headed north.

After a few silent and increasingly unbearable moments had elapsed, Stella felt safe in succumbing to her husband's charms. Without a word, she sat up and removed her black cotton shirt, revealing a black lace brassiere.

"Pretty fancy moving gear."

"A girl has to be prepared for every possible situation."

"Oh, you're definitely prepared." Nick gazed admiringly at his wife's ample bosom. "Makes me think I should thank you for that too."

Stella leaned back on the mattress. "For the lace bra or for being prepared?"

"For what's in the lace bra—and for being full of surprises." He lay down beside her and brushed her hair away from her neck. However, before he could place his lips there, the knocking sound returned, this time with greater force.

Nick bolted upright. "Okay, so I was wrong—that wasn't the house settling earlier."

"So much for no one dropping by. Bet you're glad I put that blanket up now." Stella sat up and searched for her T-shirt.

"No, no," Nick waved his hand. "Don't get dressed. Stay exactly as you are. I'll get rid of them and then be right back."

He pulled his shirt over his head and strode down the hallway and into the farmhouse kitchen. Through the back door window, he could see a woman huddled beneath the shelter of the back porch roof. Tall, thickset, and in her mid-fifties, she wore a pair of faded jeans and a Vermont T-shirt topped by an oversized corduroy shirt, and her crown of gray-flecked, dark curly hair was in dire need of a trim.

Nick opened the unlocked door, his face a question.

"Maggie Lawson. Live in the farmhouse out on the main road." Without so much as a smile, she thrust a plastic-wrapped plate of toothpick-studded chocolate cupcakes at him. "Thought I'd bring these to ya and say hello. You Graham Buckley?"

Nonplussed, he took the plate in his left hand and shook her hand with his right. "Uh, yeah. You can—you can call me Nick, though. Um ... how did you know my name?"

"Clyde down at the store told me." The identity of this Clyde or the location of said store was unknown to Nick, but Maggie apparently did not find it necessary to elaborate. Instead, she peered nosily over his shoulder. "Where's your wife? Sarah, is it?"

"Stella," he corrected. "She's, um, she's lying down. It's been a rough few days, as you can imagine."

"Can't say I can. Lived here my whole life; never moved. Wouldn't know where to begin if I did."

12

"Yeah, that's pretty much how we felt too. A little … a little over-whelmed …" In response to Maggie's blank stare, Nick's voice trailed off, and he smoothed the back of his short-cropped hair. "I'd—um—I'd show you around, but I don't want to wake my wife. She's a light sleeper. But maybe another day you can come over for coffee?"

Maggie's round face registered neither enthusiasm nor disapproval. "Yup," she replied blandly before turning on the heel of a pink perforated rubber garden shoe and heading toward the back steps.

"Thanks for the cupcakes," Nick added as she left.

"Yup."

The rain had intensified and was now accompanied by a stiff wind. Fearful that Maggie's terse responses were brought about by perceived rudeness, Nick called after her. "Hey, do you want a ride home? It's coming down pretty heavy."

"Nope. Gonna get wet putting the cows in the barn anyhow." She raised a hand in what was most likely a farewell but might have passed as a demand for silence.

"Yeah, I guess you will … won't you?" he replied, but it was too late. She had already disappeared around the front of the house.

Plate still in hand, Nick shut the back door and returned to the living room where Stella, having stripped to her underwear, sat by the fire sipping champagne.

"Who was that?" she asked as he entered the room.

"Our new neighbor, Maggie. She brought us these," he said and handed her the plate.

"That was nice of her. Mmm, chocolate," Stella lifted the plastic and sniffed. "But I thought our nearest neighbor lives over a half mile away."

Nick plopped onto the air mattress and picked up his beer bottle. "She does," he confirmed before taking a swig.

"Oh. That's odd. I didn't hear her car pull away."

"She didn't have one. She walked."

"She walked a half mile in the pouring rain?" Stella asked incredulously.

Nick answered in Maggie-fashion: "Yup."

"You're joking." Stella deposited the plate of cupcakes on the floor and rushed to the window. Taking care to remain covered, she peered from behind the blanket and watched as the figure of Maggie Lawson wended its way down the puddle-laden driveway. "She's soaked through. Didn't you offer her a ride home?"

"I did, but she wouldn't take it."

"Well, now I feel bad about not meeting her. Did she seem disappointed?"

Nick shrugged. "Hard to tell."

"Hmm. What did you tell her I was doing, anyway?"

He grinned. "That you were lying here half-naked, waiting for me to make wild, passionate love to you."

Stella gasped and ran from the window. "You did not!"

"I did. Now get over here and make sure I didn't tell that poor soaking-wet woman a lie."

She approached the air mattress, but as she did so, she noted a gummy substance on her hands. "That plate must have had some icing on the bottom of it. My hands are all sticky. I'll be right back."

"Hurry," Nick instructed as she ran out of the living room, down the hallway, and into the small lavatory off the kitchen.

She switched on the hot-water tap and waited as the long-dormant pipes sputtered, rattled, and hissed back to life before issuing forth a steady stream of cloudy red water. Stella allowed the tap to run for several seconds in an attempt to flush any impurities from the plumbing system; however, every fresh drop of water seemed just as murky as the first.

"Nick," she called. "Nick, there's something in our water."

"Did you let it run?"

"Yes, but it's getting worse."

"That can't be," he called from the living room. "The home inspector had it tested—everything checked out okay. The well guy was just here to put in a new pump. He probably didn't let it run long enough afterward."

"I don't care how long he let the water run, there's still something in it that shouldn't be there," Stella insisted. "Come see for yourself."

Nick sighed noisily and rose from his spot on the air mattress. "Stella, it's an old house. There's probably rust in the pipes that got shaken loose by the increase in water pressure. If you'd just let it run—"

"It's not rust, Nick," she interrupted, her voice rising in alarm.

"What do you mean, it's not rust?"

"I mean it's *not rust*. Look!"

Nick stuck his head in the bathroom door and immediately saw the cause of his wife's concern. The water, albeit clear in spots, was darkened by swirls of a viscous crimson substance. "You're right. That's not rust. It looks like—"

"Blood," Stella boldly completed the sentence. "It looks like blood."

Chapter

2

WINDSOR COUNTY SHERIFF Charlie Mills was a quiet man with quiet habits. Living in a small house on a dead-end road just outside of town, he shunned the modern-day "necessities" of satellite radio and cable television and, although dogs were *de rigueur* amongst his hunting buddies, Mills opted instead to share his quarters with Roscoe and Rufus, a pair of orange tomcats who, aside from being self-cleaning and self-exercising, also boasted the inability to bark.

Calm and steady, but with enough personal quirks to enable him to communicate with the area's more fringe inhabitants, Mills was precisely the sort of man one would call upon to resolve a dispute or to take charge during an emergency. Off the job, his slow, deliberate mannerisms made him the ideal fishing and hunting companion, and his taciturn nature made him a favorite audience for the loudmouths and braggarts who gathered at the local bar.

Mills's understated personality had gone far in helping him win the friendship and respect of every person in town, with the exclusion of one. And she was the only human being in all of Vermont that Mills actually wanted to impress.

Alma Johnson, Miss Maple Syrup of 1973 and Queen of the Prom for the graduating class of 1974, had been the object of Charlie's affection since he had first laid eyes on her in the cloakroom of Miss Betsy's morning preschool class. Blue-eyed, raven-haired, and with a wit sharper than the best deer-cleaning knife, Alma would eventually grow to possess an hourglass figure that would have made Raquel Welch go green with envy.

To state that Alma Johnson could have had her pick of any man in Windsor County and several towns beyond was no exaggeration. It therefore came as a great surprise to her Vermont neighbors when Alma, at the tender age of eighteen, eloped to Keene, New Hampshire, with Russell "Rusty" Deville.

Ten years Alma's senior, Rusty Deville was a junk dealer who talked big, drank big, and did very little except to chase down car wrecks and attractive women. It was during one of his frequent cross-border auto-part scavenges that Rusty first encountered a bikini-clad Alma bathing at the local swimming hole with her high-school friends.

Like countless men before him, Rusty was instantly taken with the dark-haired beauty. But the why and wherefore behind Alma's decision to even speak to Rusty, let alone fall in love with and marry him, to this day had yet to be explained. Some townsfolk theorized that Alma, in her youth and innocence, had simply fallen victim to Rusty's smooth-talking salesman ways. Others speculated that Alma, fresh out of school and with no prospects for college, saw Rusty as a way to get out of town and escape her abusive father.

Whatever her motive, Alma married Rusty just six weeks after their swimming-hole meeting, and she bore him a son one year later. Dark-haired and blue-eyed, Russell James Deville Jr. possessed both his mother's wit and good looks. However, he also inherited his father's tendencies toward laziness, drunkenness, lechery, and dishonesty.

Upon completing high school on the five-year plan, a drunken Rusty Jr. celebrated at a friend's graduation party, where he proceeded to try to force his attentions on his host's girlfriend. The girl in question managed to extricate herself from the situation before it escalated into rape and fled, shaking and bruised, to her boyfriend, who by this time was also very drunk. Before she could finish her story, the boyfriend pulled his father's hunting rifle from the living room gun case and shot Rusty right in the heart. Rusty died five days later, and his friend, despite feeling great remorse and regret, was convicted of voluntary manslaughter.

With the death of her son, Alma lost any reason to continue with pretense. Her marriage, as well as any of the original feelings behind it, had faded long before Rusty Jr.'s untimely demise. So, precisely a week after burying her only child, Alma packed up her belongings, moved into a one-bedroom apartment in downtown Keene, and filed for divorce.

In the years that followed, Alma lived a solitary existence. Swearing off the dating scene, she bought an African gray parrot for company and spent her weekends watching movies and baking cookies and cupcakes for the children in her apartment building. During the week, she worked any job she could find that didn't require a college degree. But as she approached her fiftieth birthday and saw her youth and her employability waning, she knew that she had better come up with a better plan, and fast.

With the attainment of a university-level education financially out of reach, Alma decided to pursue a career doing the thing she loved most: baking. Expanding her repertoire of cookies and cakes to include breads, pies, and pastries, she quickly discovered that not only did she enjoy working with flour, sugar, eggs, and yeast, but she seemed to possess a natural talent for it.

The universe must have agreed, for several months into her great baking experiment, Alma received word from her brother, Raymond, that Grandma's Donut Hole, their hometown coffee shop, was closing after thirty years of business. Seizing a chance to start life anew, Alma moved back home and, with Raymond's help, converted Grandma's into Alma's Sweet Shop.

Using the freshest ingredients from local farms, Alma's menu featured muffins, scones, cakes, breads, tarts, pies, quiches, and, of course, coffee and doughnuts from Grandma's original recipe. The business was an immediate success. Six mornings a week—Alma's was closed on Sundays—one could find its retro chrome-trimmed counter lined with everyone from truckers and construction workers to schoolchildren and senior citizens. However, one occupant of its red upholstered swivel stools remained constant.

From the moment that Alma's Sweet Shop had opened its doors for business and for every morning afterward, Sheriff Charlie Mills had been the first customer of the day. Waking in the wee hours of the morning and driving fifteen miles out of his way in all sorts of weather, Charlie ensured that, Monday through Saturday, he was outside Alma's door the moment she unlocked the deadbolt and flipped the Closed sign to Open.

Although the painted lettering on the Sweet Shop door designated seven AM as the official start of business, there had been occasions when Alma, knowing that Mills would be waiting in knee-deep snow or the subzero winds of a Vermont winter, had unlocked the door prior to his arrival and greeted him with his usual: two straw-berry-filled doughnuts and a cup of coffee with cream and sugar.

It wasn't befitting of a law enforcement officer to look forward to hazardous weather, but Mills relished those inclement mornings alone with Alma. There in the shop with the front door sign still turned to Closed, they would sip coffee, listen to the school-closing announcements, and reminisce about the snow days of old.

In the three years since she had returned to town, those early snowy mornings were the most intimate moments Mills had ever shared with Alma, yet they had done little to establish a true rela-tionship between the two. For when the snow had stopped and the sun returned and the crowds lined up at the Sweet Shop door, Mills's presence once again elicited nothing more from Alma than a smile, a nod, and a quick thank you.

Acutely aware that his early morning doughnut routine had produced little aside from an expanding waistline, Mills purposely parked his patrol car at the end of the Buckley's driveway, adjusted the plastic on his wide-brimmed hat, turned up the collar on his state-issued rain slicker, and, despite the driving rain, began a brisk walk toward the old farmhouse.

Red-cheeked and winded, he arrived at the side yard of the house and brushed past the fresh-faced officer who, with a tangle of windblown yellow tape, was trying to cordon off the property. "What have we got, Lou?" Mills asked of the non-uniformed man who stood beside the Buckleys' early 1900s well.

Louis Byron, Windsor County coroner, pulled the hood of his green Carhartt rain jacket over his gray head and pushed the bridge of his glasses farther up on his nose. "Allen Weston."

"The owner of Weston Wells and Pumps?"

"Yup, and Weston Waste Removal and Speedy Septic Service."
Byron led Mills to a gurney upon which lay a black body bag.

"Yup, doing okay for himself."

"He was." Byron unzipped the bag to reveal the contorted body
of Allen Weston. Clad in a red flannel shirt stained with both blood
and mud, the eyes and mouth of the dark-haired, bearded man
remained open in a lifeless expression of surprise.

"Snapped his neck?" Mills asked.

Byron shook his head. "Shot in the chest—three times, as far as I
can see, but I'll tell you more when I get him back to the lab."

"Guess we can rule out suicide, then."

"Yup. Unless you reckon it likely that he drove out here, shot
himself, and threw the gun away before he fell down the well."

"Drove," Mills repeated under his breath. He scanned the area
for a sign of Weston's vehicle but found none. "I don't see a truck
anywhere. Was there one when you got here?"

"Nope. If he had one on the property, it wouldn't leave tracks.
Been too dry."

"Yup. First rain we've had in, what, two weeks?"

"'Bout that."

"How long you figure he's been down there?"

"Well, I figure he's been dead four, five, maybe six hours, but he
didn't die right away. Too much blood. The concrete well cover's
been lifted off and the pump's been shut off, leaving just the surface
groundwater."

"Weston was probably servicing it," Mills interjected.

"Yup. New owners claimed they had blood coming through the
line, and there's still a fair amount down there. If I had to guess—

and it is a guess—I'd say he was there at least a couple hours before he died."

"So then he was shot, say, seven to nine hours ago?"

"Yup. Sounds 'bout right," Byron replied. "But again—"

"You'll know more when you can take a good look at him," Mills completed the sentence. "I know, Lou. I know. This ain't exactly our first rodeo."

"Sure as hell right about that, Charlie. Say, when are you gonna retire anyway?" Byron teased.

"You first, Lou," Mills volleyed before heading into the farm-house.

Chapter

3

FULLY DRESSED, STELLA sat on the air mattress, her chin resting upon her hands, and watched as Nick poked the dying embers of the fireplace. "I can't believe it. You and I have lived in the New York City area our entire lives. That's over seventy years of urban living between the two of us, and not once in that time did we even come close to encountering a dead body. We're in Vermont for less than a day—in a town where, supposedly, no one even locks their doors—and suddenly we have bloody water in the sink and a dead body in our well."

"I believe that's what's known as irony," Nick theorized.

Between the call from Shelburne and the discovery of the body in the well, Stella couldn't help but wonder if someone or something wasn't sending them a warning. "Is it irony or is it just a bad omen? I know you've been looking forward to this move, but what if this isn't the right time to be moving? What if this isn't the right house?" she asked as tears streamed down her face.

Nick leaned the poker against the brick of the fireplace and sat down beside his wife. "Hey, come on, now. I admit that when we first found that guy's body, I wondered if maybe this place wasn't jinxed. But then I pulled myself together and realized that his death was just an accident. An unfortunate accident."

"An accident that took place the same day we moved in."

"The timing sucks, I know, but I'm sure this sort of thing has happened elsewhere before. Working on a well as old as ours must come with its fair share of risks. One false move and—"

"But nothing has gone right today, Nick," she sobbed.

He slid an arm around her shoulder and pulled her closer. "Come on, now, that's not true. The move, the trip here, and the closing all went without a hitch. It even waited until we got here to rain. If anything, I'd say we've been pretty lucky."

"Lucky?"

"Yeah. We're alive, and we have each other. That's more than the dead man and his family have right now."

Stella suddenly felt like a selfish fool. "You know, as much as I love the way you make me laugh, there's something to be said for your more serious moments. Sometimes you really know how to put things in perspective."

"Thanks." He hugged her and kissed the top of her head. "My only wish is that we knew about the body earlier."

"So we could have saved him?"

"That, or we might have been able to shave a few bucks off the price of the house."

Stella freed herself from his embrace and punched him playfully in the arm. "Or—here's a thought—we could have bought a house that *didn't* come with a dead body?"

"Is that a search option on those real-estate websites? 'Corpses not included?'" he smirked.

"It should be. It seems just as important as an eat-in kitchen or an en suite bathroom."

"At the moment, I'd say it's more important."

Stella and Nick's musings were interrupted by the appearance of a man in the living room doorway. Short and stocky, his reddish beard was flecked with white whiskers, and his eyes, although a cold blue in color, conveyed a gentle wisdom. Beneath his open raincoat, the buttons of his uniform strained slightly against his middle-aged paunch.

"Sheriff Charles Mills, Windsor County Sheriff's Office," he introduced himself. "You're Mr. and Mrs. Buckley?"

"That's right," Nick confirmed as he rose to his feet. "I'm Nick, and this is my wife, Stella."

Mills shuffled through the forms on his clipboard. "Nick? Says here your first name's Graham."

Be it her good-girl suburban upbringing or her love of the film *My Cousin Vinny*, there was something about being questioned by a small-town police officer that made Stella feel uneasy. Charm was her only defense. "Nick is his nickname. Get it? *Nick*name?" she laughed nervously.

Mills failed to crack a smile.

"Thanks, honey. I haven't heard that one since sixth grade," Nick quipped to his wife before answering the sheriff's question. "The name Graham will get you beaten up pretty quick in a New Jersey schoolyard, so I started going by my middle name, Nicholas—Nick for short."

"That where you two are from? Jersey?"

"No, Stella grew up on Long Island, and we lived in the city seven years before moving here."

Mills's eyes slid to the air mattress and its snarl of mismatched blankets. "You got into town yesterday?"

"No, today," Stella stated flatly. "Just a few hours ago."

Mills glanced, in turn, at the air mattress, the champagne bottle, Nick, Stella, his wristwatch, and again at the air mattress. "So about four o'clock," he suggested, the color rising slightly in his cheeks.

"Yeah, around then," Nick grinned.

"And did you notice anything strange when you arrived?"

"No, I don't think so. Did you notice anything, honey?"

"Hard to say, since I'm not sure what normal is around here. Oh! Not to say that you people aren't normal—um, Vermonters, I mean"—Mills raised an eyebrow—"but, um, if you mean normal as in did the place look the same way it did the last time we saw it? Then yes. Yes, it was normal."

"The body in the well belongs to Allen Weston, owner of Weston Wells and Pumps."

"That's the company that was supposed to install the new well pump," Nick stated.

"Then you knew Allen Weston?"

"Never met the guy."

"Did you speak to him over the phone?"

"We had been advised to have the old well filled in and drill a new one," Stella jumped in. "But what with the closing and moving fees, we honestly couldn't afford to do it. So the seller agreed to pay for a pump upgrade just so that we'd pass inspection. He's the one who hired Weston—actually, since he lives out of state, he got the real-estate agent to handle everything on his behalf."

Mills looked around appreciatively. "That's right. This is the old Colton place, isn't it? How is good old Barry anyway?"

"No idea," Nick answered. "We didn't meet him either."

"Huh? Well, I guess the lawyers take care of everything now, don't they? Yup … last I heard of Barry, he was living in California, working at some highfalutin' computer place. He still there?"

"Our closing documents list him as living in Colorado," Stella said.

"Colorado. Is that right? Guess our mountains were too small for him … hmph." Mills scratched the back of his head and tried to regain his train of thought. "So, you never met Allen Weston, but you knew that he was going to be here today."

"We knew someone from his company would be here, yes," Nick corrected. "We didn't know it would be Weston himself until yesterday."

"Oh?"

"The pump was originally going to be replaced yesterday afternoon, but I got a call from the real-estate agent—"

"What's his name, by the way? This real-estate agent?" Mills interrupted.

"*Her* name," Stella corrected, "is Alice Broadman. She's with Vermont Valley Real Estate."

"Go ahead," Mills instructed Nick, with a nod of the head.

"Anyway, Alice called me yesterday to say that the appointment had been moved to this morning, and that due to the last-minute cancellation and the urgency of the situation—we were closing this afternoon—Mr. Weston would be installing the pump himself."

"Did she tell you why the appointment had been changed?"

"No. She just assured me that the new pump would be installed and tested before the end of closing."

"Tested," Mills pondered aloud. "Weston would have needed to run the taps inside in order to test the new pump. Was Alice Broadman going to meet him here to let him in?"

"No. She was busy with the closing and some errands I had asked her to run for me. She asked if it was okay for her to stop by here first thing in the morning, unlock the door for Weston, and then have him lock up when he was finished with the work."

"Is that what you did?"

Nick shrugged. "The house was empty. I didn't see a problem with it."

"Was the house locked when you got here?"

"Ye—" Nick started to answer but then recalled his visit with Maggie Lawson. "Wait—the front door was, but the back door wasn't."

"It wasn't?" Stella asked from her spot by the fire.

"No. I didn't think much of it at the time, but it was definitely unlocked."

"Are you sure?"

"Positive. I clearly remember opening the door to talk to Maggie, and all I did was turn the knob."

"Maggie?" Mills questioned. "Maggie Lawson?"

"Yeah, she lives up on the main road. She's our nearest neighbor. She came by to introduce herself."

"Yep, that's Crazy Maggie. When I first got the call I thought it was trouble at her place. Didn't think it was here."

"Crazy Maggie?" Stella echoed.

"Yup, that's what we call her. She's a strange 'un."

"Strange how?"

"Just plain ol' strange—no other way to say it. She's pretty harmless, though, so long as you don't get her riled up."

"What happens when you rile her up?"

"Well, she pret' near came at Mrs. Colton with a shotgun once. And Ray Johnson says she poisoned his dog."

"Poison? She gave us cupcakes. I licked the icing off my fingers when I found out I couldn't wash my hands!"

"Idn't give much thought to that. If Maggie's mad at you, she'll let you know about it, and she sure as heck wouldn't be bringing you cupcakes."

"That's comforting," Stella said sarcastically as she stood up and moved beside her husband.

"So the back door being left open," Nick returned to the business at hand. "Why is that important?"

"Helps us figure out the time of death. From that, we can work out where everyone was at the time."

"Where everyone was at the time?" Stella repeated as she envisioned her and Nick behind bars. "You mean like an alibi? I thought this was an accident. I thought Weston fell down the well."

"Oh, he fell down the well, all right. He fell down 'cause he was shot."

Nick stepped forward. "Someone shot him? You mean this is murder?"

"Can't say just yet. Could be an accident. Black bear season just started."

"Black bear season?"

"Turkey and deer too, but that's just bow and arrow hunting for now."

"Yeah, I work for the US Forest Service. I know when the seasons take place," Nick said impatiently. "What I'm saying is, how does someone mistake a guy in a red flannel shirt for a bear?"

"Shooter didn't have to see him. When a hunter misses what he's aiming at, just where do you suppose those bullets go?"

"I guess you're right. It could have been a stray bullet that got him."

"A stray bullet, sure, but Sheriff Mills said *bullets*," Stella spoke up. "How many times was Weston shot?"

"You can find out in the paper tomorrah," Mills replied quietly. "Until then, why don't you tell me how you happened to find Weston's body."

Nick and Stella described the bloody tap water and their subsequent actions.

"I thought an animal had gotten into the well," Nick explained. "I've seen raccoons climb into chimneys and storm drains to escape predators, so I figured a wounded raccoon or woodchuck crawled into the well to hide and then bled out."

"Realizing that the only way an animal could have gotten into our well is if the cap had been left off," Stella reasoned, "I called Alice to get the number of the well company to complain, but she had already left for the day."

"So," Nick picked up where Stella left off, "I got a flashlight from the glove compartment of our car and went out to take a look."

"I was right behind him," Stella inserted.

"Yes, you were, honey. You were stuck to my arm like Krazy Glue," Nick noted with a raise of his eyebrow. "I flashed the light into the well expecting to see a dead fox, but instead I saw a man dressed in a red flannel shirt."

"Buffalo check," Stella offered.

"That's the first thing I noticed about him—that bright red shirt. He was stuck about two-thirds of the way down, and he was obviously dead."

"What do you mean 'obviously'?" Mills inquired.

"He was blue."

"Blue?"

"Well, bluish gray," Stella amended as she placed a hand on her husband's shoulder. "At least his lips and his face were. Probably from lack of circulation. Rigor mortis. Cyanosis. All those things you see on *CSI*."

Mills knitted his eyebrows together and scratched his head so intensely that his hat lowered over his eyes. "*CSI*?"

"Yeah, you know, the crime scene investigation show? Blood that glows in the dark and all that stuff."

Before Mills could explain that he did not own a television, a woman appeared in the doorway of the living room. Tall and slender, she looked as if she had just stepped from the cover of *Country Living* magazine. A ruffled plaid shirt topped by a brown leather blazer draped her delicate torso, and her narrow waist and long legs were hugged by a pair of dark-wash jeans. A pair of flat brown boots finished the look on the bottom, and on top, her long, dark hair had been gathered into a tight braid.

Stella watched as Sheriff Mills sucked in his considerable gut.

"What's going on here?" the woman demanded.

"Ms. Deville, how did you get in?" Mills countered, his heretofore unflappable demeanor now somewhat less composed.

"Simple. I walked up the driveway and opened the front door."

"No one tried to stop you?"

"No. Why should they? They know who I am."

Mills sighed in exasperation. "Why are you here?"

Ms. Deville raised her left arm to display a finely woven basket, the contents of which were obscured by a red-and-white-checked napkin. "I came to welcome this young couple with a few sandwiches and cookies. That's my famous seven-grain bread and my prize-winning oatmeal raisins," she whispered to Stella with a smile and a wink. "But I can see that the sheriff's office has already sent out the welcome wagon."

"Can't discuss it, Ms. Deville. Official police business," Mills replied in an overly gruff tone.

"Stop calling me Ms. Deville, Charlie. We've known each other since we were in diapers. It's Alma," she stretched a hand to Nick. "Alma Deville. I own the Sweet Shop in town. You'll find a coupon in that basket too—good for 10 percent off any baked good."

"Nick—Nick Buckley, and this is my wife, Stella. Thanks for the food . . . and the coupon."

"Oh, don't thank me for that. I feel terrible using a social call to drum up business, but these days, a girl has to market herself when she can. Sometimes she even has to be a bit of a bitch." She took Stella's hand. "Now tell me, why is the sheriff here bothering you? You seem like nice people to me."

"Alma," Mills warned.

"Charlie, you know gossip in these parts travels faster than a tick to the hindquarters of a dog. Once those men of yours get home and tell their wives and girlfriends, the news will have spread from here to the Northeast Kingdom. Not much sense in keeping me in the dark."

With a weary sigh, Mills capitulated. "All right."

"There's a dead man in our well," Stella blurted.

"What? You're pulling my leg."

Nick shook his head.

"Do you know who it is?" Alma turned to Mills.

"Allen Weston," the sheriff replied.

The color drained from Alma's face. "Allen Weston?"

"Yup. You, uh, knew him from the shop, didn't you?"

"Y-yes. He—he had been in a few times and he, um, he emptied my septic tank last summer."

"Oh?"

"Well, he didn't, but his crew did. Weston never handled the field work. Not that he couldn't, mind you," she added quickly, "but he was more focused on the business end of things. Speedy Septic didn't live up to the speedy name by any means, but they got the job done. Hank Reid, however, had all sorts of trouble. They tried to empty his septic tank in the middle of mud season, and the dang thing floated up out of the ground. Poor Hank called in Jake Brunelle to replace all the pipes. Cost him thousands, which Hank doesn't have—or at least he'd like us to think he doesn't have it, what with the way he keeps that house of his."

"A regular trip down memory lane," Mills remarked. "He must get a decent pension from the school, though. He worked there as a janitor all his life."

"Mmm," Alma agreed. "So what happened? Did Allen fall into the well and break his neck?"

"He was shot," Nick stated.

"Shot? You mean he was murdered?"

"Could have been an accident," Mills once again asserted.

"Not if someone didn't report it. You remember that case in Jacksonville a few years back? The kid was tried for second-degree murder because he left the man wounded and crying for help."

Mills raised an admiring smile at both Alma's memory and her understanding of the legal system. Smiled, that is, until he recalled that her knowledge stemmed from personal loss. "He sure was."

"And, despite all the guns out there, fatal hunting accidents don't happen as often as you'd think. So either way, this is gonna wind up as a murder investigation," Alma announced and then folded her arms across her chest triumphantly. "So you still gonna claim you're looking into an accident?"

"Nope. I'm gonna ask you all to leave."

"Leave? But this is our home," Stella argued.

"You can come back once we do what we need to do. Until then, you'll have to stay elsewhere."

"But Weston was shot outside, by the well," Nick spoke up. "Why do we have to leave the house?"

"Weston's body might have been found out in your yard, but we don't know for certain he was shot there. That open back door gave Weston, or his shooter, full run of the place. Heck, if it was premeditated, the shooter could have been waiting in your kitchen. Now look," Mills's face softened. "I know you folks are eager to move into your new home, but I can't let you trample over potential evidence. I promise we'll try to wrap things up quick. Until then, Alma can help you find a motel—"

"Motel?" Alma interrupted. "Why, Charlie Mills, it's nearly Columbus Day—you know the whole state's overrun with leaf-peeping flatlanders!"

"Flatlanders?" Stella asked.

"Oh, all the people who come here from New York and New Jersey and Connecticut and think they own the place."

Stella flashed Nick a worried glance.

Alma drew a hand to her mouth. "Oh, I am sorry! I didn't mean the two of you! I mean the folks who come up here and block up the roads with their SUVs, expect traffic to wait for them when they walk into the middle of the road, and pollute the place with noise and trash. By the end of the season, you'll be sick of 'em too. My point was that inn and motel rooms are as scarce as hen's teeth right now. But don't you two worry; I can put you up, at least until deer season starts."

"I thought it already had."

"No, that's bow and arrow deer season," Mills explained. "Alma's talking about deer rifle season, which is the second week of November."

Stella couldn't envision shooting deer with anything other than a camera, but she kept her opinions to herself. "It's very sweet of you to put us up at your place, Alma. Thank you so much. I promise we won't inconvenience you for long. As soon as we can get a room elsewhere, we'll be out of your hair. Right, Nick?"

"Absolutely. Once the flatlanders are finished decimating the town, we'll check into whatever decent motel is still standing. Unless, of course, we're able to move in here by then."

"Oh, you're not gonna be in my hair at all," Alma said pleasantly. "Our place is barely big enough for me and my brother, Raymond. No way I could fit another person in it, let alone two. But Raymond has a hunting camp just a few miles from here. It's just one room, and it's not winterized, but it's not so cold at night that you two can't manage. What do you say?"

Stella and Nick once again exchanged worried glances before replying in unison, "Hunting camp?"

Chapter

DECIDING THAT IT was easier to leave the moving truck at the farmhouse than to attempt to steer it through the woods surrounding the hunting camp, Nick and Stella retrieved their suitcases from the truck's cab, flung them into the back of Alma's black Ford F-150 pickup, and followed her back through town in the Smart car.

Lined with a mix of two-story brick storefronts and white clapboard buildings, Teignmouth's Main Street was the quintessential New England thoroughfare. Marble sidewalks and granite curbs provided pedestrians with a safe path between the many shops and eateries. A center median separating the two lanes of traffic had been planted with rows of yellow and rust chrysanthemums.

Indeed, Teignmouth could easily stand in for the setting of one of Norman Rockwell's famous paintings. Stand in, that is, if the sparkling white sidewalks and the newly paved road weren't awash with rain, swarms of tourists, and close to one hundred idling automobiles.

The brake lights on the F-150 glowed red in the gathering twilight as Alma slowed behind the long queue of cars that clogged

Main Street, all of which bore license plates from places other than Vermont. She thrust her head out of the driver's-side window and motioned to the Buckleys to do the same.

Nick rolled down his window.

"See what I mean? Two weeks every October. Two weeks! And Sheriff Mills thought you'd get a hotel room. Ha!" she shouted before pulling her head back inside the cab of the truck.

Nick closed his window and wiped the raindrops from his face. "She's right. This is like midtown during rush hour."

"Or any day the president is in town."

"Gridlock for the president, I understand," Nick complained. "But these people are here to look at *leaves*."

"I don't understand it either. The traffic wasn't this bad when we drove through this afternoon."

"Probably because it wasn't raining then. And it wasn't supper time."

"Ah, yes. Feeding time at the zoo," Stella noted sarcastically.

The two vehicles traveled at a snail's pace through the bumper-to-bumper traffic before finally turning onto a side road that led to a dark, empty section of Route 4. After driving fifteen miles, they turned left onto a narrow dirt road that cut across the nearly thirty acres of pristine woodlands that surrounded Raymond Johnson's hunting camp.

During daylight hours, the scene was undoubtedly breathtaking, but without the sun's glow or even a street lamp to illuminate their brilliant reds, yellows, and oranges, the local sugar maples, yellow birches, ashes, and elms blurred together, forming an inky black canopy against the starless evening sky.

"Where the heck is this place?" an eager Stella asked from the passenger seat. "It feels like we've been driving forever."

"It's a hunting camp, honey. You're not going to find it alongside a strip mall," Nick explained as his knees banged and scraped against the dashboard with every twist and bump in the road.

Nick seldom drove their car. Whereas Stella's job sometimes required her to travel to museums in the outlying boroughs, Nick's position at the US Forest Service's New York City Urban Field Station had been a short subway ride from his and Stella's Murray Hill apartment building. And, while most of Stella's friends had married and settled in the suburbs, Nick's buddies either lived locally or just over the bridge in New Jersey.

The decision to purchase an automobile was therefore entirely Stella's, and the moment she spotted the bright yellow coupe, she fell in love. Fuel-efficient, easy to park on crowded city streets, yet youthful and trendy in appearance, she thought it the ideal vehicle for an urban couple in their mid to late thirties. Nick, on the other hand, was left wanting more—of everything. Likening the experience to piloting an airplane from a coach seat, Nick was never comfortable driving the Fortwo. Indeed, even its bright yellow color had spurred him to dub the car "the pee-mobile." Yet, for the sake of marital harmony, he agreed to the purchase and silently suffered through taking Stella on the odd shopping trip or visit to his mother-in-law's.

However, when Nick's friends, upon seeing their buddy wedged behind the tiny two-spoke steering wheel, dubbed him Magilla Gorilla, Nick declared to his wife that although he was still available to drive the Fortwo when needed, he fully intended on purchasing a manlier automobile just as soon as their finances would allow.

"Looks like we're here," he announced as he threw the transmission into park and immediately stretched out his arms.

The high beams of both the truck and car shone brightly upon a single-story house with a front porch. Clad with unfinished wooden planking, the weathered gray exterior of the structure was punctuated in the front by a solid door and two mismatched windows. In the rear of the building stood a small shed, and in the front yard area sat three Adirondack chairs and a wooden table with two metal spikes that stuck up from either end.

"This is camp?" Stella questioned. "I expected to see tents."

"Seriously?" Nick looked at her and shook his head.

"Why not? When my friends used to go camping, they brought tents and sleeping bags."

"This is a hunting camp, not a Boy Scout jamboree. The guys who use this place aren't making s'mores."

"Whatever," Stella shrugged. "It's a pleasant surprise, at least. An actual house instead of a big tent. And look, there's even a picnic table. Now that it's stopped raining, we might be able to drink our coffee out there in the morning. We'd have to be careful where we put our cups, but still..."

"Those spikes are there because that's not a picnic table, it's a skinning table."

"A skinning table? What's—" Stella was about to ask what a skinning table was when its purpose suddenly became clear. "Oh! That would explain why there are no benches with it, wouldn't it?"

"Yeah, it kinda would." Nick exited the driver's-side door and, flashlight in hand, helped Stella out of the passenger side before leading the way to the front door, where Alma stood waiting.

"Here we are," she declared as she opened the front door. "Hunter's paradise!"

"I can't see anything," Stella stated. "Where's the light switch?"

By the dim light of her flashlight, Alma managed to find her way inside. "This is our light switch," she stated as she ignited a red cigarette lighter. Placing her flashlight on a nearby surface, she held the lighter beneath a dangling white object and reached into the darkness with the other.

Within moments, the white object glowed with a light similar to that of a standard 60-watt bulb.

Nick recognized the source immediately. "Gas lamps, huh?"

"Of course. Can't get electricity out here."

As Alma lit the rest of the gas lamps, the remainder of the room became visible. Approximately eleven feet wide and seventeen feet deep, the cabin was rustic in every sense of the word. Sheets of particle board bearing traces of dirt, blood, and other unidentifiable substances served as flooring, while the ceilings—if they could be called that—consisted only of bare rafters naked of both plasterboard and insulation.

A corner of the back wall had been fitted with one white hanging cupboard, one knotty pine base cabinet with sink, a two-burner stove, and a large metal cooler to serve as a makeshift cooking area. Meanwhile, the front portion of the space was furnished as a living room, replete with a duct-tape-plastered avocado green recliner, a collapsible snack tray that subbed for an end table, and a threadbare sofa upholstered in a bicentennial-era "Spirit of '76"-themed fabric.

Stella felt as though she had stepped into the basement on *That '70s Show*, but she remained positive and gracious. Given the current lodging situation, she was glad to have a roof—even if it were uninsulated—over her head. "Quite cozy. Where's the bedroom?"

"You're standing in it," Alma replied with a nod at the sofa. "That there's a pull-out bed. Don't know if there's sheets on it, but I have some blankets in my truck."

"We brought our blankets too," Nick quickly interjected, "so we should be fine. Right, honey?"

"Absolutely. All I really want right now is to eat those sandwiches you fixed, have a hot shower—"

"Oh, there's no shower," Alma corrected. "The only water out here is from a gravity-fed spring. Ice cold and hard enough to turn your blond hair bright green. If you want to get cleaned up, stop by my shop in the morning. I'll give you the key to my doublewide."

"Your what?"

"My doublewide trailer. Raymond and I are both out of the house by six, so there'll be no fighting for the bathroom," she explained with a smile.

"A shower would be terrific. Thank you, Alma."

"Yeah, thanks for your help," Nick added. "I don't know where we would have gone if you hadn't stepped in."

"Ain't nothing," Alma dismissed with a wave of her hand. "Now if you'd just grab your suitcases outta my truck, I'll get going and let you folks rest up."

Stella and Nick followed Alma to her truck, retrieved their suitcases, and after a few words of parting, went back inside the camp.

"Well, this isn't quite where I expected to end our day," Stella sighed.

Nick set the flashlight on the snack table and instantly burst into laughter.

"What? Why are you laughing?"

"Never in my wildest dreams did I ever think you'd wind up sleeping in a hunting camp."

"Believe me, I had no intention of proving you wrong. But you know what? I can make do for one night. Sometimes it's good to step outside your comfort zone."

"Uh-huh. And after the one night?"

"I'm a smart woman. I'll figure out all this wilderness stuff."

"I'm sure you will." He laughed even harder. "Even though you thought we'd be sleeping in a tent and singing campfire songs."

"I did not! Well, okay, maybe I did expect a tent, but not a Girl Scout sort of thing. I imagined something closer to what you'd see at an archeological dig or a nature photo shoot, not," she began to chuckle, "my grandma's rec room in cabin form. Seriously, everything in here dates to the Ford administration."

"Hey, don't knock it," Nick said and flopped onto the couch, his hands behind his head. "My parents had a sofa like this when I was growing up. Used to bring girls back to the house to watch TV and, you know…"

"Yeah, I know." Stella rolled her eyes.

"I tell you, between my brother and me, that sofa saw a lot of action."

"I'm sure it did. Maybe not as much action as you told people"—Nick glared at her—"but I'm sure it had its fair share. Just don't expect to re-create any of those make-out sessions tonight—at least not until you throw a few blankets over that thing."

"Don't worry, you're safe. Nothing puts a damper on the mood like discovering a corpse."

"Ugh. Don't remind me." She shivered and picked up the flashlight from the snack table.

"Where are you going?"

"The outhouse. I haven't gone since the closing."

"Want me to go with you?"

"No, I can manage on my own."

"Are you sure? It's pretty dark out there."

"I have the flashlight, and, aside from the outhouse, I know where everything is." She pulled the hood of her sweatshirt tightly over her head and set off through the front door.

It didn't take long, however, before the sounds of the wind, rustling leaves, snapping twigs, and unseen woodland creatures left Stella wishing she had taken Nick up on his offer. She paused and deliberated turning back, but the knowledge that her sudden reappearance would be met with Nick's mocking laughter urged her forward.

Sticking close to the perimeter of the house, Stella followed the length of the side exterior wall until she was a few yards away from the outhouse. Her flashlight trained upon the door of the structure, she stepped carefully through the tall grass until she reached her destination. With tentative fingers, she turned the rusty latch.

What awaited Stella inside the outhouse was, to her urban sensibility, more horrifying than anything she might have encountered during the walk from the cabin. With no lights, no sink, and no modern fixtures, the single-room building consisted only of a small ventilation window located near the roofline and, along the far wall, an enclosed wooden bench into which had been cut a large round hole. Beside the hole sat a roll of toilet paper.

Stella scanned the bench area with her flashlight in hopes of discovering a handle, chain, or some other device by which to flush the wooden toilet. Upon finding none, she sighed heavily. *Well, when in Rome,* she thought to herself.

Putting her flashlight down on the bench, she began to undo the top button of her jeans only to look up and see a large white eyeball with a dark brown center staring through the window.

Stella reared backward and bumped into the bench, causing both flashlight and toilet paper to topple into the dark abyss of the latrine. Screaming at the top of her lungs, she lunged for the door, her fingers fumbling frantically for the latch. Before she could locate it, the door suddenly swung inward, hitting Stella in the face and sending her careening to the floor.

Now silent, Stella looked up to find Nick standing in the doorway, holding a kerosene camping lantern. "Oh, Nick," she exclaimed as she sprung to her feet. "It was a peeping Tom! He was looking in the window."

"A peeping Tom in the middle of thirty acres of forest?"

"But it was!"

"He must have been about seven feet tall to be able to look in that window."

"I-I-I don't know, but I saw him! He looked right at me."

"Yeah, I saw him too. It was a buck."

"Who? What? His name is *Buck*?"

Nick laughed. "No, a *buck* as in a male deer. I came out to make sure you were okay, and I spotted him looking into the outhouse."

"Whew," she cried in relief. "Well, the good news is, I don't need to go to the bathroom anymore. The bad news? I need to put on another pair of underwear."

Nick grinned and shook his head in disbelief. "Go grab your flashlight, and we'll go back inside."

Stella nodded in agreement and turned around to grab the flashlight off the bench. "Uh-oh."

"What?"

She pointed to the hole in the bench, which was now glowing eerily from inside.

"How did you—? Aw, never mind. Good thing I brought this along." He held the lantern aloft.

"You're my hero."

"Yeah? You won't say that when I send you to fish that flashlight out tomorrow," he teased.

"Fish it out? I was thinking of adding lights to all our toilets. That way you'd know where to aim in the middle of the night."

"Keep it up and you won't be using a net."

Playfully bickering all the way, the couple picked their way through the pitch-black darkness of the Vermont forest and settled into the cabin for sandwiches and sleep.

Chapter 5

AFTER FIGHTING A seven-hour battle with the lumpy, blanket-covered sofa bed mattress, Stella and Nick admitted defeat and yielded to the coming daylight. Bleary-eyed, they gargled with a generous amount of mouthwash, performed some rudimentary hairstyling, and, armed with a bag filled with shampoo, conditioner, and fresh clothes, drove their tiny yellow car through the fog and rain to Alma's Sweet Shop.

Located in a corner brick building on Main Street, the Sweet Shop was proof that even restaurant style was cyclical in nature. Boasting original pink Formica countertops and tables in a boomerang pattern and upholstered swivel stools and benches of red vinyl, the Sweet Shop interior attracted both older patrons looking to stroll down memory lane and younger customers who were intrigued by its retro appeal. Meanwhile, white Swiss dot curtains, hand-lettered signs, and quilted placemats—all Alma's handiwork—promised diners of all ages an eating experience as pleasant, unique, and friendly as the proprietor herself.

Nick opened the heavy glass door to the sound of sleigh bells and ushered Stella inside. With the exclusion of Sheriff Mills and Alma, the eatery was empty.

"Hey, you two," Mills greeted.

Alma, sporting jeans, a sweater, and a ruffled floral-print apron in colors that matched the shop's décor, emerged from behind the counter and welcomed the couple with open arms. "Good morning, my dears. How'd you sleep?"

"Oh … great," Nick replied with a yawn.

"Never slept better," Stella joined in and took the counter seat beside Sheriff Mills.

Alma returned to her post. "Liars. That sofa bed has more loose coils than a Slinky factory."

Nick hopped onto the stool beside his wife. "It's not that bad."

"Yes, it is. I love that camp for two things: the scenery and the quiet. As for everything else? Disgusting at best. Strictly man town." Alma poured two mugs of steaming hot coffee and shoved them toward Stella and Nick. "Unfortunately, I couldn't think of any place that isn't full for the weekend."

"Don't worry about it—it was still better than sleeping in the car." Stella stirred milk into her coffee. "I was just surprised by the amount of traffic here in town last night. If I hadn't seen it, I would never have believed a town could get so many tourists on a Thursday."

"At this time of year, Thursday's the start of the weekend."

"Last night weren't nothing," Mills jumped in. "By this afternoon, you'll think twice before setting foot into town."

"Yup, while the leaves are changing, the only true weekdays are Tuesday and Wednesday."

"Are you saying we won't be able to get a room until Tuesday?"

"Probably not. Town is packed."

Sheriff Mills nodded his head in confirmation.

"Seems quiet now," Nick noted.

"That's 'cause it's only quarter to seven. I'm not even supposed to be open yet." Alma presented them with two menus. "How 'bout some breakfast? This lists our cooked-to-order items, and baked goods are listed on the board behind me."

"How come I never get a menu?" Mills complained as he took a bite out of a sugar-studded jelly doughnut.

"You used to, but since you order the same thing every day, I figured I'd save my energy."

"If you're not open yet," Stella asked, "then how were we able to get in?"

"'Cause I feel bad when my first customer of the day, every day, has to wait out in the rain."

"You come here every day at opening?" Stella asked the sheriff.

Sheriff Mills blushed. "Yup. Wanna be the first to taste Alma's excellent coffee."

Stella took a sip from her white earthenware mug. Alma's coffee was serviceable, but one could have purchased a similar cup from the Stewart's convenience store down the road. Given his reaction to Alma's arrival at the farmhouse, she was willing to bet that there was an ulterior motive to Mills's patronage.

Nick placed his menu facedown on the counter. "I'll have the breakfast sandwich on your seven-grain bread."

"I'll have a cranberry-orange scone," Stella ordered, her mind more focused on the matter of accommodations than on breakfast.

"So, Sheriff Mills, since we obviously can't find a room in town, what's the chance that we'll be able to stay at the house tonight?"

Mills frowned and shook his head. "Slim to none."

"By then, you and your men will have had twenty-four hours to give the place a thorough search. Isn't that enough time?"

"Haven't gotten the coroner's report yet. Until we do, we don't know what we're looking for."

Nick spoke up. "You don't need a coroner's report to tell you that Weston was shot."

"Nope. But I do need it to tell me what he was shot with, where the shot might have been fired from, and whether or not his body was moved."

"When will you receive the report?" Stella inquired.

Mills took a sip of his coffee and swallowed. "Afternoon, most likely."

"Once you get it, can you use the information to search the living room first? That way, maybe if it checks out okay, we can …?"

"Mrs. Buckley, I'm gonna be blunt. Even if an initial search of your house comes up clean, I'm not gonna let you folks go rushing back there. Not 'til I know who did this."

"What if we stayed in one room—just to sleep—and didn't touch anything else? We'll even promise to be out of there by morning, so your men can do whatever they need to do."

"Sorry, but someone shot Weston and left him to die. Until my case against that person is tighter than the bark on a tree, I'm not taking any chances."

"I understand. I'm sorry for pushing you, Sheriff. It's just…" her voice trailed off.

"No need for apologies. I understand you're eager to set up housekeeping, and I feel bad you two got more than you bargained for. But, as much as I'd like to let you folks move in, I know that cutting cross-lots might come back to bite me in the a—ahem, butt—later on."

Stella's eyes narrowed. "'Cutting cross-lots?'"

"Taking shortcuts," Alma paraphrased as she served up the Buckleys' breakfasts.

Nick lifted the top slice of bread from his sandwich and sprinkled the filling with a generous amount of black pepper. "If we can't stay at our place, can we at least get our air mattress?"

"I knew it!" Alma exclaimed. "You hate that sofa bed as much as I do."

Nick grinned sheepishly.

"Was the air mattress at the house when Weston was fixing your well?" Mills asked.

"I don't know. Probably."

"Then the answer's no. I want everything in that house to remain as it was and where it was until I can sort things out. Besides, I don't think you wanna be over there today." He pushed the morning newspaper in front of Stella's plate.

Stella looked up from her scone. Stamped in big bold letters across the front page of the *Rutland Herald* were the words *Local Contractor Found Dead in Well*. Beneath the headline, a few short paragraphs described the body's discovery, the subsequent police activity, and the community's reaction. Set inside the article was a photo of the late Allen Weston. Dressed in a dark gray suit and matching tie, the ends of his mouth were turned slightly upward into a smile that was partially obscured by his neatly trimmed black beard.

She stared at the photo for several seconds. The image of the smiling, well-dressed businessman stood in such stark contrast to the scene at the bottom of the well that Stella found it difficult to reconcile the two.

"If the *Herald* already has the story, you can bet that every reporter within a two-hundred-mile radius is gonna be on your front lawn this morning. You two show up saying you own the property, and that sofa bed won't be the only thing keeping you awake."

"But it doesn't say in this article the address of where his body was found. All it says is a farmhouse well."

"They don't need to say where," Alma asserted. "This is a small town. All those reporters need to do is drive into town and ask. For a few bucks, they'll find plenty of people more than happy to point the way."

"I don't think we want to live with that type of celebrity," Nick remarked in between chews. "Do we, honey?"

Stella didn't answer. Her attention was still riveted on the newspaper photograph. "I heard you talk about his businesses yesterday, but what else do you two know about Allen Weston?"

"What do you mean?" Alma asked as she unlocked the shop door and flipped the Closed sign to Open.

"I mean that if this wasn't an accidental shooting, then we're dealing with a case of murder. You live in the same town as Weston did. Do you know why someone might have wanted him dead?"

"I don't engage in gossip, Mrs. Buckley," Mills chided.

Alma returned to her spot behind the register. "I don't either. It's not good for business."

"Okay, let's try approaching this from a different angle. You both met Weston, right? What did you think of him?"

"Good businessman," Mills replied instantly.

"Smart," Alma answered immediately after the sheriff. "Very smart."

"Well, he was the owner of three successful businesses; I think both those descriptions go without saying. But what was Weston, the man, like? Where was he from? Did he have family? What did he believe?"

"Why do you want to know all this, Mrs. Buckley?" Sheriff Mills challenged.

"I don't know. I guess I'd just like to get to know the man who died in my well."

"He was from Jersey, for a start."

"Jersey?" Nick spoke up. "Huh, somehow I got the impression that he was a local."

"Nope. Moved here ten years ago or thereabouts. Divorced, I think."

"Yep, he was divorced," Alma confirmed. "No children though."

"Weston started the pump company right away. It was just him in those days. He ran the office and did the work. No employees. He weren't a friendly sort, but he showed up on time and always answered the phone—when you've been here longer, you'll realize how rare that is. It weren't long before business picked up to the point he was able to hire few men. A little bit after that, he bought out Mack Lawson's trash removal business, and then, a few years later, Speedy Septic."

"Mack Lawson? Any relation to Maggie Lawson?" Nick asked.

"Maggie's husband. Now deceased."

Stella had taken a bite of her scone, but this bit of news caused crumbs to spew from her mouth. "Maggie—the person you called Crazy Maggie—was *married*?"

"Yup. Mack was pret' near crazy as Maggie. A hoarder. He'd pick through his customers' trash, looking for things that might be valuable."

"He swore someday he'd be on one of those antique shows on TV," Alma added with a loud cackle. "The trailer Mack used for an office looked like the set of *Sanford and Son*. I can't even imagine what their house looked like."

"Mack had always sifted through people's trash, looking for treasure. For years, he'd pick up the trash in the morning, bring it back to his office, and sort through it before dropping it at the dumps. But then he got the bright idea that it was quicker to sift through the bins while they were still outside his customers' homes. As you could imagine, that didn't go over well."

"A lot of Mack's customers were second homeowners—owned big ski lodges and condos up on the mountain," Alma explained. "They had no idea that Mack had been picking through their trash."

"And when they caught wind of it, they gradually left," Mills went on. "Weston was able to buy the business—trucks, office, dumpsters, everything—for a song. In fact, he got the whole thing so cheap, he bought Speedy Septic later that year."

"Mack was never the same after he lost the business," Alma concluded. "He passed away shortly afterward."

"Sounds like Maggie had a reason to hold a grudge against Weston," Nick said.

"Yes, but once again we're back to Weston the businessman," Stella argued.

Alma's face grew hard. "Because that's the only way Weston could relate to people. He didn't socialize, and he only took part in community events if they offered him publicity. He could be charming when he needed to be—very charming. But otherwise, he was a cold man. Cold and calculating."

"Yup, Weston made sure he always got what he wanted. And if he didn't," Mills's eyes slid to Alma, "he took it."

Before Stella could comment, a short, heavyset man entered the shop and approached the register. He reached a stubby, callused hand to the visor of his red trucker's hat in greeting. "Two coffees to go, Alma."

"Sure thing." Alma nodded and set to work filling two tall cardboard cups.

"Well, if it ain't Jake Brunelle," Mills welcomed.

"Mornin', Charlie. Surprised to see you here. Thought you and your boys would be busy fishin' Allen Weston out of a well."

"Guess you saw the paper, then."

"Nope. Clyde at the store told me. What happened? Someone give him a shove?"

"In a manner of speaking. He was shot."

Jake Brunelle's darkly bearded face registered neither horror nor surprise. "Hmph. Prolly a hunter going after black bear or someone shootin' deer when they ain't supposed to."

"Probably right. But either way it's manslaughter."

Alma plunked the two cups of coffee onto the counter and covered them with plastic lids.

Brunelle thrust a plaid-covered arm into the pocket of his stained denim overalls and extracted a fistful of bills. "Well, it weren't me, if that's what you're getting at. I was putting in a septic tank over at the Upjohn's farm. You can give 'em a call if you want."

"Thanks, Jake. I will. I didn't want to have to ask you where you were, but knowing just how much you like bear meat and how much you hated Weston, I couldn't help but wonder."

"Good thing I set that straight, then." He selected a few wadded dollars from the wrinkled pile and slid them across the counter to Alma. "See you at camp next weekend, Charlie?" he asked as he picked up the coffee cups.

Before Mills could reply, a petite woman in her mid-forties rushed through the door. She was dressed in a trendy but inexpensive purple gabardine raincoat, a paisley scarf, and a tight-fitting pair of skinny jeans finished with a pair of high-heeled ankle boots. Her shoulder-length brown hair, although neatly trimmed and styled, sported blond highlights of so many shades and thicknesses that it was apparent the color originated from a box and not a salon. The layers of foundation, powder, and mascara she had applied to her face were a bit heavy for daytime wear. Yet, despite her ill-chosen attempts to retain her youth, it was obvious that this woman had been, and still was, quite pretty. "Jake! What's taking you so long?"

"I was just talking to Sheriff Mills here."

"Oh, hello, Sheriff. I'm sorry. I didn't see you sitting there."

"Mornin', Betsy. How are you?"

"Okay, thanks, but in a bit of a hurry." Betsy turned to her husband. "We'd better get moving if we're going to make it to that estimate by eight o'clock."

"Yeah, I know. I'm comin'," Jake rolled his eyes. "See ya, Charlie."

"See ya, Jake. Bye, Betsy."

The couple hurried from the shop, their presence immediately replaced by a pair of young girls who took the two stools at the far end of the counter.

Following the Brunelles' lead, Nick pulled his wallet from his jeans' back pocket and slid the 10 percent coupon toward Alma.

"Oh, no," she pushed the coupon back. "This one's on the house. Least I can do for making you sleep on that bag of coils last night."

"If it weren't for that bag of coils, we'd have nowhere else to spend the night," Stella stated.

"Tell you what, you can use the coupon tomorrow morning. How's that?"

"We'll be here," Nick promised.

"Wait! I almost forgot." Alma rushed to the cash register and returned with a piece of paper that she promptly passed to Nick. "These are the directions to get from here to my house. I printed them off Google. Never did that before—I'm so proud of myself."

"You should be. Um … do we need a key?"

"Nope, it's open. Always open. Just go in, get cleaned up, watch the TV if you'd like. Make yourselves at home." The sleigh bells on the front door heralded the arrival of three men dressed in work jackets and baseball caps. "I'd best get to my customers. See you tomorrah."

As Nick and Stella slid from their stools and zipped their jackets, Mills slapped a ten-dollar bill on the counter and, with a tip of his hat, bade farewell to Alma before following the couple out of the shop.

The morning's heavy rain had dissipated, allowing the Buckleys to walk back to their car at a more leisurely pace than the one they had assumed walking away from it. Sheriff Mills, parked a few cars behind them on the street, kept pace. "Looks like it might be clearing. Good thing about New England: if you don't like the weather, just wait—" Mills fell silent as he stared at the Buckleys' yellow vehicle. "What is that?"

"Our car," Stella answered.

"*Her* car," Nick replied simultaneously.

"What are you going to do with it?"

Stella opened her eyes wide. If the sheriff couldn't figure out that a Smart car, although small, was still a functioning automobile, she and Nick might still be homeless come deer season. "Um … I don't know. Drive it?"

"Not in winter, you're not. You'd have a better chance of pushing a mule a mile uphill than getting that thing in your driveway."

"I'm planning on getting a truck," Nick explained. "A big truck. Might even be able to get one from the job."

"Good thinking. Hey, since you folks don't have nothing but a camp stove, you might want to head down to the Windsor Bar and Grill later for burger night. Five bucks gets you a big, juicy burger with fries and the fixin's. It's a local hangout, so no leaf peepers or yellow plates, and they don't skimp on the meat either."

"Yellow plates?"

"New Jersey folk." Mills realized his error. "Oh, I'm sorry. I didn't mean to—"

"That's okay. I get it. Flatlanders aren't allowed."

"Well, if they happen to know the sheriff, they are."

"Sounds good. We might just have to check into that."

"I'll see you there," Mills said with a wave before heading off for the white-and-red squad car.

As Nick approached the car, the keyless entry system unlocked both doors, allowing himself and Stella to climb inside.

"So? What do you think?" she posed as soon as she had fastened the passenger-side seat belt.

"Five-dollar burgers? Hey, I'll give it a shot. Sounds like the sheriff wants to meet us there, but that's not necessarily a bad thing. He seems like a decent guy and—who knows?—maybe he'll have some good news for us by then."

"I wasn't talking about burger night. I was referring to the conversation prior to that."

"What, the car? I don't know. If we can get snow tires for this thing, I'm sure it'll be fine in the driveway. Our property's pretty flat. I still want to try and get a truck through work. It'll come in handy for hauling lumber and house stuff. Besides, it would be nice for each of us to have a vehicle during the day."

Stella slapped her hand to her forehead and sighed noisily. "All right, not the previous conversation but the previous *previous* conversation. The one about Weston."

Nick raised his eyebrows. "Oh yeah, that whole Alma speech about Weston being cold was kinda weird. I mean, she hired the guy to work on her house. How would she know he was cold, and why would she care?"

"Particularly when he wasn't even around to do the work."

"That's right. Alma said yesterday that his guys performed all the labor. Apart from the sale, when did she have the chance to interact with him?"

"Uh-huh. Makes you wonder if he pumped more than her septic tank, doesn't it?"

"Pumped her septic tank? Jeez, and to think I kiss that mouth before I go to sleep each night."

"Oh, you love it."

Nick pulled a face and nodded slowly. "Yeah, I kinda do."

Stella glanced at the side-view mirror. "Mills is still parked behind us. Maybe we should get going?"

Nick complied by putting the key into the ignition and turning it. The sound of the three-cylinder engine was barely audible. "Why? Are you worried he'll give us a ticket for loitering?"

"No, I just don't want him to see us talking."

"Couples talk all the time."

"They do. But Mills's comment about Weston taking what he wanted didn't sit well with me either."

"Yeah, that was kinda creepy."

"Turn right at the next light," Stella directed. "Yeah, it was creepy, but what really bothers me is his insistence that Weston's death might have been the result of a hunting accident. Even though Mills asked Jake Brunelle for an alibi, it seemed somewhat forced, didn't it? Like he didn't actually believe he needed to ask."

"Mills is probably being conservative. He's not going to make a big deal about it until he receives the coroner's report. Besides, the guy's been around a while. He must have seen other accidental shootings. Maybe this matches up to what he's seen before."

"Okay. If this was an accident, where's Weston's truck?"

Nick made the designated turn and, having witnessed Mills driving past their turnoff, pulled the Smart car onto the shoulder of the road. "It should have been at the house, where he was killed."

"But it wasn't. Why not?"

"I don't know. Maybe someone drove off with it, or—"

"Or Weston was shot elsewhere, and his body was thrown down the well," Stella stated.

"But either scenario would suggest that the shooter was covering his tracks."

"Exactly," said Stella. "Which doesn't really fit with the stray bullet theory, now, does it?"

"Do you suspect the sheriff of something?"

"So far, nothing aside from loving Alma Deville."

"The sheriff? And Alma?" Nick uttered in disbelief.

"I'm not saying they're an item. I don't think Alma even has an inkling of Sheriff Mills's feelings, let alone reciprocates them."

"How can you be so sure he has feelings for her? He seems to treat her like anyone else."

"Oh, come on. Did you see him suck in his gut yesterday? And that whole 'being the first to drink Alma's coffee' excuse was pretty lame. He goes there every morning, before anyone else arrives, to see her. The guy's got it bad."

"Can't say I blame him. She is an attractive woman. But what, if anything, does that have to do with Weston's death?"

"I don't know. Maybe nothing. Or maybe she's the reason he keeps insisting this is an accident."

"First Mills has the hots for Alma. Now he's covering up for the fact that she murdered Weston. Don't you think you're jumping the gun?"

"Absolutely," said Stella. "That's why I think we should talk to some of the townspeople and get their perspective on things."

"Uh-huh. So why the sudden Nancy Drew routine?"

"What are you talking about?"

"I'm talking about you noticing men sucking in their guts, questioning our new neighbors—oh, and investigating an accidental shooting you believe to be murder."

"I'm not playing Nancy Drew. Part of a curator's job is solving mysteries. Not only do I figure out the background of a tapestry, what it depicts, and how it fits into history, but when restoration is required, I need to determine what pieces are missing and how to re-create them. I need to fill in the blanks."

Nick paused. "And that's why you feel the need to fill in the blanks surrounding Weston—because you're a curator?"

"That's part of it, but the main reason is that the sooner we can fill them in, the sooner we can get back into our house and on with our lives."

"I want to move in as badly as you do, Stella, but I'm not sure we should be getting involved in police business."

"We're not getting involved, we're just talking. Besides, what else are we supposed to do with our day?"

"I don't know. Take in the scenery, catch up on some reading, and if you feel like filling in blanks, we can try to find a needlepoint shop. You can make something for the new place," he suggested.

"I have canvas and supplies in my suitcase; I plan on starting a new project tonight. But needlepoint is a hobby. It's meant to help me unwind at the end of the day; it's not supposed to help me fill it. That's what a job is for."

"That's what this is really about, isn't it?" Nick shifted the car into park and placed a comforting hand on his wife's shoulder. "I know you're worried about the job hunt, but don't lose faith, okay? Finding Weston was upsetting at best, but like I said yesterday, that doesn't mean that our luck has changed or that the rest of this move is doomed. You still haven't heard from Shelburne. They could call any day now to say that you have the job."

"They already did call."

"What? When?"

"Before closing. On the ride up here." Her eyes welled with tears. "They gave the position to someone else."

"Oh, honey, I'm sorry." He leaned across the center console and took her in his arms. "Why didn't you tell me?"

"I didn't want to ruin the day," she replied between soft sobs. "You were so ... you were so looking forward to this."

"I still am. This is just a stumbling block."

"It feels like more than that. It feels like the bottom just dropped out of everything. We have no idea of when we'll be able to move into our house. And the job ... I put so much stock into that position, but I guess I just don't have what it takes."

Nick put his hand under her chin and tilted her head back so that their eyes met. "That's really why you're snooping, isn't it? Not only are you looking for a distraction, but you're trying to prove to yourself that you have what it takes."

"I also feel as though there's a whole part of me that I haven't had a chance to explore. Although I love being a curator, I only became one because my mother pushed me toward the arts. What if I'm not supposed to be one? What if the Shelburne job is a sign that I'm meant to be doing something else?"

"So you're wondering if you're supposed to be a detective like your father?"

"Maybe. I don't know. I seem to be questioning everything right now, and, although it sounds ridiculous, I just can't help but think that by making sense out of this whole Allen Weston thing, everything else will fall into place."

Nick drew a deep breath and waited several seconds before speaking again. "So, where first?"

Stella wiped her tears and grinned broadly. "You mean it? You'll help me?"

"Someone has to make sure you don't get mistaken for a black bear, and who better for the job than a US Forest Service employee? Besides, while you were talking, I realized something."

"What?"

"That all the books I've been meaning to read are boxed up and sitting at the back of the moving truck. That leaves my day pretty much open, so I'll ask again: where first?"

"I'd like to pay a visit to Alice. After we shower, of course."

"Yeah, I could use some cleaning up," he agreed and pulled the car back onto the road. "I can't believe we slept in a hunting camp, are going to shower in a trailer, and are going to be investigating a dead body in our well. The whole thing just seems surreal."

"I know. Here we thought we'd be moving to some quiet little Vermont hamlet where people die of boredom. But instead..." Stella placed a hand on Nick's knee and started to laugh.

"What is it?"

"Remember in *Midnight in the Garden of Good and Evil* when John Kelso describes Savannah as *Gone with the Wind* on mescaline? I'm beginning to think that this place is *Peyton Place* on Wild Turkey and maple syrup."

Chapter
6

LOCATED IN AN old Victorian home on the edge of town, Vermont Valley Real Estate had suffered greatly during the recent housing crisis. In 2004, when the market was at its peak, the two-story building accommodated six agents, two secretaries, and a receptionist. Today, the second floor had been rented out as an apartment, and the only individuals working on the main floor were an aged, somewhat cantankerous receptionist and Alice Broadman, the agency's owner.

"Why, if it isn't the new kids in town," Alice exclaimed as she rose from one of four desks in the room. Short and squat in stature, Alice's makeupless face, mousy brown hair pulled tightly into a bun, and wardrobe of ill-fitting pantsuits and sensible shoes made her appear far older than her thirty-six years. "How's the house?"

"We'll let you know as soon as we're able to move in," Nick quipped.

Alice brought her left hand to her mouth, revealing a plain gold wedding band. "It *was* your place! Tim, my husband, heard the story on VPR this morning and asked if that's where Weston was found. I said it might be. Most houses these days have new wells just a few inches wide. Can't fit a dead body down them, unless it was eaten by a python," she giggled.

"What's VPR?" Stella asked.

"Vermont Public Radio. They broadcast news in the morning and then switch to classical music for the rest of the day." Upon noticing that the gray-haired receptionist was watching them intently, she quietly waved Nick and Stella into a nearby conference room.

"I hate that old nosebag," Alice asserted as she shut the door behind her. "She's always listening in on my conversations. I should probably fire her, but even in this economy, I'd never find anyone else willing to work for what I pay her."

Pulling a padded Windsor chair away from the large maple table, Alice sat down and gestured for her guests to do the same. "So, where did you guys stay last night if you weren't allowed in the house? I can't imagine you got a room here in town—not during foliage season."

"Ray Johnson's hunting camp," Stella replied as she positioned herself across the table from Alice and alongside Nick. "Alma set us up."

"Oh, I love Alma's! Did you eat there this morning? Her cinnamon rolls are wicked good."

"We didn't have the cinnamon rolls. We'll have to try them tomorrow. Right, honey?" Stella turned to Nick and smiled; Alice had provided the perfect segue to discuss the murder.

"Sure, although that breakfast sandwich I had was pretty tasty. I might—"

Stella kicked him in the shin. They hadn't come here to discuss breakfast foods, but the scent of Alma's baking still resonated. "*Tomorrow* we'll try the cinnamon rolls. You can have your breakfast sandwich another day. I'm sure you'll have plenty of opportunity since it doesn't look as if we'll be having breakfast in the new place for a while."

Thankfully, Alice took the bait. "Why won't you be having breakfast in the new place? Surely you must be allowed back in by now."

"Actually, no, we're not. Not until Sheriff Mills gets this case wrapped up."

"What's there to wrap up? Allen Weston fell into the well. It was an accident, right?"

Stella debated the proper course of action. The papers and the radio hadn't mentioned Weston's gunshot wounds, but that was in all likelihood due to the lack of a coroner's report. Once the official findings were released, everyone in the state would know that Weston hadn't died of a broken neck. Assuming, of course, that they hadn't already heard the news from Jake and Betsy Brunelle.

Seeing no point in delaying the inevitable, Stella decided to tell Alice the truth. "It may have been an accident, but it wasn't the fall that killed him. Weston was shot."

If Stella had anticipated a reaction from Alice, she was sorely disappointed, for the woman exhibited not a shred of emotion. Nick, on the other hand, stared at his wife as if she had lost her mind.

Stella narrowed her eyes at him to signal that she knew what she was doing. "You don't look very surprised, Alice."

"Well, that sort of thing happens all the time around here. It's fall, isn't it? Seems every year someone gets himself mistaken as a bear or a turkey or a deer. And it's usually because somebody's been drinking. There's a reason deer camp is sometimes called beer camp."

Stella recalled Alma's words from the previous day: *fatal hunting accidents don't happen as often as you'd think*. And yet both Alice Broadman and Jake Brunelle automatically assumed that Weston's shooting had been accidental.

As Stella pondered the possible significance of Alma's words, Nick continued the conversation. "Beer camp … I like that. The only problem is that Weston wasn't hunting when he was shot. He was working on our well."

"I know. I made the appointment. But you do realize that your farmhouse is surrounded by woods, don't you? Someone could have been hunting close to your property line and have hit Weston with a stray bullet."

"First of all, it would have been nice of you to mention the risk of getting shot by hunting crossfire *before* we bought the house."

Alice's pale cheeks turned bright crimson.

"Second, we already thought of the stray bullet theory. However, Weston wasn't shot once; he was shot three times. I'm no hunter, but I'm willing to wager that even Mister Magoo would have landed at least one of those bullets into his target—unless, of course, that target was Weston."

It was Stella's turn to be surprised. For someone who seemed eager to play things close to the vest, Nick was showing all his cards.

"Then there's the matter of Weston's truck."

"What about his truck?"

"It wasn't at the farmhouse when we discovered Weston's body."

"It wasn't? It was there when I dropped off the air mattress and champagne."

"Are you sure?"

"Positive. The well service trucks are bright yellow; Weston chose that color so that they'd stand out from the other contractor trucks in the area. One of his genius marketing schemes."

"Did you see him or just the truck?" Stella quizzed.

"No, he was there. I didn't speak to him though," Alice added hastily. "He was outside talking on his cell phone."

"Outside? Is that because the house was locked?" Nick spoke up.

"No. I know most contractors start work at eight o'clock, so I stopped by a little before then to unlock it. Don't think I had to, though. Weston didn't even have the cap off the well when I got there."

"What time was that?"

"Oh, ten thirty or so."

Stella remembered how Alice, flustered and frantic, had arrived late to their twelve-thirty closing. "What time did you leave the farmhouse?"

"By the time I inflated the air mattress, probably about a quarter after eleven."

"And Weston was still on his phone when you left?"

"N-no, but I was in a rush. I had some phone calls to make before your closing, so I left without talking to him." The color once again rose in Alice's cheeks. "W-why are you so interested in my whereabouts?"

"I'm not. I'm just trying to get a timeline on Weston's death."

"Don't you think you should leave that to the police?"

"Oh, I plan to. But, you see, Nick and I are a bit bored. We had planned to use these few days to unpack and get settled. But now that we're on hold, well, there's not much to do except to join in the local gossip."

The comment had the desired effect. Alice's face became more relaxed. "That will definitely keep you busy. Behind maple syrup, lumber, and cheese, gossip is our biggest product."

"Yeah, we've noticed," Nick joined in. "Our neighbor knew my name before I even introduced myself."

"Your neighbor? Oh, you mean Crazy Maggie. Yeah, news spreads fast. Not always accurately, but fast. I'd say it was like the game of telephone, except that most of the news is usually passed along in person. Church suppers, pig roasts, maple sugar week-ends... the highlight of them all is the gossip. Oh, and never stop at Perkins if you're in a hurry. Clyde will stop whatever he's doing just to listen to a juicy story. I went there once to pick up ice cream, and by the time he finished talking to Irma from the post office and rang up my order, the whole gallon had just about melted."

"So that's who Clyde is," Nick said under his breath.

"Pardon?"

"Nothing. Since we're gossiping, I was just wondering what you've heard about Weston. I mean, I'm a city boy: jaded and cynical to the extreme. But even in the city, when a guy dies, you're going to find someone—even if it's just one person—who has something good to say about him. But from the article in the *Herald*, it seems the nicest thing anyone can say about Weston is that he was a good businessman."

"Because that's all he was," Alice stated plainly. "Maybe he meant more than that to someone out there, but I can almost guarantee that person doesn't live in these parts."

"Wow," Stella remarked with a smile. "Was he as popular as that?"

"Pretty much—or pret' near, as a true Vermonter would say. Weston was brusque and arrogant, which doesn't sit well in a place like this. People here pride themselves on being down-to-earth."

"What about other businesspeople? What did they think of him?"

"Some respected him. Others got rubbed the wrong way."

"And you? Did you ever do business with Weston?"

"Only to take care of your well. I would rather have hired Jake Brunelle, but Mr. Colton, the seller, insisted on calling Weston to do the job. And since he was paying, I wasn't in a position to argue."

"That's the only time you dealt with him? Weston never used your services as a real-estate agent?"

"He was more interested in taking over other business than in buying property."

"But he must have bought a house when he moved into town. Didn't he use you to—"

"He built his house on land he had purchased decades earlier," Alice interrupted. "I wasn't an agent then, but if I had been, he'd have been out of luck. It would have been a cold day in hell before I signed any piece of paper that had Allen Weston's name on it."

"That's a pretty strong sentiment," Nick noted.

"Allen Weston wasn't known for his fairness and honesty," Alice said bluntly. "I worked hard to build my business. I wouldn't want his reputation to rub off onto me."

"Reputation? So Weston had dealings with other people in town?" asked Nick.

"Yes, but I'd rather not implicate anyone by mentioning names."

"No need. We understand you wishing to protect their privacy."

"Although," Alice's pale eyes sparkled with new life, "it's no secret that Weston's employees didn't think much of him."

"Oh?" Stella leaned back in her chair, confident that her one-syllable response would spur Alice onward.

"Apparently, he cut their wages—which you might expect in the middle of winter, when the well and septic businesses were slow, but he did this right in the middle of summer. Summer! And then there's that whole Josh Middleton business."

"Josh Middleton?" Nick inserted on cue.

"He worked for Speedy Septic. Young kid with a criminal background, which is pretty much what you'd expect of someone who pumps out tanks for a living."

During the course of her and Nick's home search, Stella had come to think very highly of Alice. But the narrow-minded remark about Josh Middleton's criminal background spurred Stella to consider that the real-estate agent might have a darker side. "Are you suggesting that Middleton might have been involved in Weston's death?"

"I'm not suggesting anything, but I wouldn't be surprised to learn that he was involved somehow. Weston had Middleton arrested a few weeks back for stealing a truck. Middleton's out on bail now, awaiting trial. If convicted, he'll get two years in prison for breaking parole."

"I could see where Middleton would be angry with Weston, but if he stole the truck—"

"But he didn't steal it. At least that's what he claims. He said Weston let him borrow it in order to meet his parole officer the next morning."

"Where was the truck when the police tracked it down?" Nick inquired.

"Parked outside Middleton's mother's trailer. He lives with her."

"That's a pretty stupid thing to do, wouldn't you say?"

"What, park a stolen truck outside your house? I wouldn't do it."

"Nor would most moderately intelligent people. So, would you describe Middleton as being none too bright?"

"No, not at all. If anything, he's one of the smartest guys Weston had working for him."

"Then I'm more inclined to believe Middleton's story than Weston's. We're talking about a septic truck here, not a Corvette. I could see Middleton taking a septic truck out for a joy ride or to play a prank, but if he's smart—and we're assuming he is—he would have taken it back to the shop afterward. I mean, what else is he going to do with it? Go trolling for girls?"

"Eww," was Stella's only comment.

"Exactly. The simple fact that it was parked outside his mother's house—er, trailer—supports his story. He wouldn't have brought the truck there; he'd have known that was the first place the cops would look."

"Middleton's mother believes his story too," Alice told them. "She's the one who raised the bail money, though I'm not sure how. She barely scrapes by as it is; without her son's income, I don't know what she'll do."

"So not only did Weston's theft charge threaten to send Josh Middleton to prison, but it caused his mother financial hardship," Stella summarized.

"Can we say *motive*, boys and girls?" Nick sang.

"I know I can," Stella said. "The question, however, is whether Middleton is the type to commit murder. I know you said he has a criminal background, Alice. What was he arrested for?"

"I don't remember—drugs of some kind. Does it matter, really?"

"Yes, it does. There's a big difference between being caught with a bag of pot and killing a person in cold blood."

"According to you, perhaps. But what about Weston's truck missing from the murder scene? Sounds like a calling card from Middleton, if you ask me."

"You think he killed Weston and took the truck as a"—Stella struggled to find the appropriate words—"thumb-to-the-nose sort of gesture?"

Alice's face registered bewilderment.

"What my wife means," Nick interpreted, "is that taking Weston's truck from the scene was Middleton's way of saying 'screw you for accusing me of stealing your truck, you filthy rotten—'"

"Nick!"

"Yes," Alice affirmed. "That's precisely what I think he did."

"And you don't think there could be another explanation?"

"Maybe, but if it weren't Middleton, it was another one of Weston's employees." She raised a stubby finger. "Mark my words: whoever bumped off Weston plotted it right under his very nose."

Chapter 7

APPROXIMATELY A HALF mile away from the white clapboard shops and well-heeled tourists of Main Street stood Teignmouth's industrial area. Separated from the rest of town by the tracks of the Vermont Rail System, the district consisted of a body shop, a feed store, the town waste disposal site, and Jake Brunelle's shop. Given the nature of its tenants, the section was more trade-oriented than truly industrial; however, that didn't prevent the town board from designating the neighborhood as Teignmouth Business Park.

Farther down the railroad tracks and just beyond "the park"— as the locals called it—stood the Wiley Campgrounds. Prior to the establishment of the park and before the revitalization of Teignmouth's town center in the 1970s, the campgrounds were a popular stop for road-weary families looking to enjoy Vermont's fresh air and breathtaking mountain views. Today, the campgrounds had become a mobile home park that acted as home to approximately seventy families and was administered by the Vermont Department of Housing and Community Affairs as part of their low-income housing initiative.

At the end of one of Wiley's many dead-end streets, twenty-two-year-old Josh Middleton sat on the wooden steps of a dingy gray trailer that overlooked the town garbage dump. Clad in a green camouflage T-shirt, ripped gray jeans, and a pair of black Chuck Taylor Converse hightops, he drew a long puff from his unfiltered cigarette before flicking the butt onto the patchy brown front lawn. "Are you some kinda detectives?"

"No," Nick said. "We just bought the house where Allen Weston's body was discovered."

"Oh yeah? Bet your place is crawling with cops. Probably as sick of them as I am."

"Not yet," Stella replied, "but we're getting there. It wouldn't be so bad if they'd just let us move our stuff in and get settled."

"They won't let you move in? Why not?"

"They're afraid we'll muck up—that's the polite term—potential evidence. The place is off-limits to everyone until they figure out what happened to Weston."

"That sucks."

"Yeah, it does. The way they're acting, you'd think *we* were the ones who shot him," Nick casually remarked.

Middleton raised a tattooed arm and scratched the back of his closely shaved head. "Shot? Paper said he was found in a well."

"He was, along with the bullet wounds that killed him."

"So that's why you're here." Middleton's brown eyes grew steely. "You think I had somethin' to do with it."

"I don't think anything at the moment, except that you might have had a very good reason for wanting Weston dead."

"Wantin' him dead ain't the same as killin' him."

"You're right, it isn't. So why don't you tell us everything that happened?"

"Yeah, right. So you can go to the cops and say you don't believe me? Nah, I ain't telling you nothin'." Middleton leapt from the makeshift stoop and reached for the screen door of the trailer, inciting the black Labrador chained in the backyard to bark madly. "I don't know why you think I'd talk to you."

"Because we're not the police. Unlike your friends at the sheriff's office, we don't think you stole Weston's truck."

Middleton paused, his hand on the doorknob. "Quiet, Luke," he shouted to the Lab. With a small whimper, Luke obeyed and lay down in front of his doghouse. "What makes you so sure I didn't steal that truck? You don't even know me. Maybe I'm as bad as everyone says."

"Maybe you are," Stella agreed. "But we can tell that you're not stupid. And that's what you'd have to be to have stolen that truck."

Middleton sat back down and stroked his chin. The reddish-blond goatee beginning to sprout there did little to diminish the youthfulness of his round face. "That's for sure. Parking it right in front of my mom's trailer. What kind of idiot do they think I am?"

"The kind of idiot who would do anything to have some fun at his boss's expense," Nick rationalized.

"I didn't have to steal a truck to do that. Besides, I liked my job. Mr. Weston could be a real dink at times, but I never saw him unless I stopped by the shop."

"And you never thought of getting even with Weston for being a dink?"

"Hey, I know where Mr. Weston lived. Great big house on a private road and a garage full of cars—expensive ones, too. If I wanted to get even, I could have broken in and taken his TV or stripped one of his cars for parts. Even at the shop, I could have walked outta there with any tool I wanted. Any of those things would've made more sense than stealing a truck full of"—his eyes slid toward Stella—"*you* know. Point is, if I had a mind to, I could have robbed Mr. Weston blind and he'd never have known it were me."

"The cops would argue that maybe you *wanted* him to know it was you."

"Where's the fun in that?" Middleton guffawed. "The best part of getting even with Mr. Weston would have been watching him go nuts. I'd have loved to see him pull his hair while he tried to figure out who ripped him off, but, like I said, I liked my job and didn't want to lose it. Couldn't afford to, neither."

"How long did you work for Weston?"

"Little over two years. Worked hard for him, too. No one ever had complaints about me."

"So it's safe to say that you were one of his best employees," Stella put forth.

"There were other guys who did an okay job, but they weren't as particular as me. I always made sure things were done right. Not so much for Mr. Weston's sake, but because my name was on it."

"Sounds like you were a valuable asset. Did Weston let you take his vehicles home on a regular basis? As a courtesy for your hard work?"

"Hell, no. Never needed them. Got my truck right there." Middleton pointed to the rusty blue-and-white pickup parked on the left-hand side of the front lawn. "Needed a new starter a few weeks back, so my mom drove me to work 'til I could get around to fixing it over the weekend. Had a parole meeting my mom couldn't take me to, so I asked if I could borrow the truck overnight and bring it back after my meeting Friday mornin'."

"And Weston agreed?"

"Yep, 'til that night, when he changed his mind and sent the cops knockin' at my door."

"I don't understand," Nick confessed. "If Weston let you borrow the truck, why did he later report it as stolen?"

Middleton pulled a cigarette from the pack in his front shirt pocket and lit it. After taking a long drag, he replied, "'Cause he wanted to get rid of me."

"If you were a good worker, why would he want to get rid of you?" Stella asked. "And if he did want to get rid of you, why didn't he just fire you?"

"You don't get it. He didn't just want me off the job. He wanted me out of the way and back in jail. That way it would look like I couldn't be trusted. Like anything I had to say was a lie."

"Why?"

"'Cause I was gonna testify in the Hank Reid case."

Stella recognized the name from Alma's story. "Hank Reid? Was that the house with the floating septic tank?"

"Yep. Back in the spring, right after the ground thawed, it rained 'bout five days straight. All that water mixed with the snowmelt to make for some pretty big floods. Me and another guy went out to Hank's to put in a new tank. Minute we got there, I knew we should wait. Half the yard was under two inches of water, maybe more. I called Mr. Weston from Reid's house and told him I couldn't do the job."

"How'd he react?" Nick questioned.

" 'Bout as good as he usually reacted to those things," Middleton grinned. "Started cursin' and swearin' and yellin' at me over the phone. Even ol' man Reid could hear him, and he weren't anywhere near the phone."

"Why would he be so angry?" Stella asked. "Didn't he realize you were trying to save him from a lawsuit?"

"Didn't matter. All he worried about was that he'd promised a golf buddy of his that we'd work on his tank the rest of the week. If we pushed Reid's job back, we'd have to push Mr. Weston's friend's job back too, or we'd have to leave in the middle of it to take care of Reid since he couldn't go much longer with the tank he had."

"Don't tell me: this golf buddy was probably someone wealthy or influential who'd be unhappy if you didn't show up when scheduled," Nick guessed.

"Yep, you got it. I even told Mr. Weston that I'd come back and dig up Hank's old tank on my own time, but he wanted it done right then and there. Warned us that if we didn't get the job done, we'd both be fired.

"Like I said before, I didn't wanna lose my job," Middleton continued, "and the guy I was workin' with, his wife was about ready to have their second kid, so he couldn't afford to lose his."

"What did you do?"

"Couldn't do much else except empty the tank and start diggin'. Didn't take more than a few turns with the backhoe 'fore the hole filled with water and the tank came floatin' to the top."

"What happened then?" Stella prodded.

"I called Mr. Weston and told him the tank had come up and all the connections most likely needed replacin'. He was madder than all hell. He said to get outta there as quick as we could. I didn't like leaving ol' man Reid with that mess, but I figured Mr. Weston was gonna send over another crew or even come over to fix it himself. That's what I would have done if it were me. I had no idea he'd write it off the way he did."

"He didn't make the repairs?" Nick said in amazement.

"Nope. Ol' man Reid had to call in Jake Brunelle to drain the hole, sink the tank, and fix the connectors. Cost him thousands to get the system up and runnin' again. Jake let him slide as much as he could, but with Mr. Weston at his back, he couldn't give his time away for nothin'. That's when Mr. Reid called a lawyer."

"Seems logical that he'd sue Weston."

"Yep, and I was glad he did 'til . . ."

"Until when, Josh?" Stella gently asked.

" 'Til I found out Mr. Weston meant to blame the whole thing on me. I was supposed to take the rap. I—I couldn't let him do it . . ."

"I understand why you'd be angry; I'd be angry too. But even if he blamed you, it was still Weston's company," Nick rejoined. "He'd ultimately be responsible for the damages."

"I know, but it's more than that. I do good work—work I'm proud of. I don't want my name mixed up with that whole deal. *I* weren't the greedy one. *I* tried to stop it."

"But Hank Reid knows that, doesn't he? You said he overheard the conversation."

"Yup, that's why his lawyer asked me to make a statement."

"And, naturally, you agreed. So Weston set out to discredit you."

Middleton nodded. "Wanna hear somethin' else? When I finally got 'round to workin' on my truck, I found out someone had messed with the starter. I figure Mr. Weston did it so I'd miss my parole meeting. He didn't 'spect me to ask for the truck. But when I did, he got an even better idea—framin' me."

"Do you have any proof?"

"That the truck was messed with? Or that Weston did it?"

"Both."

"The wires to the starter were cut. I don't know who else'd have reason to do it besides Weston."

"But you didn't see him do it."

"Nope. But I know it was him."

"And now that Weston's dead, where does that leave you?"

Middleton became oddly silent.

"Come on, man. I'm sure you already spoke with your lawyer. What did he say to you? If you don't tell us, we'll go look him up."

"He said I still have to go to trial," his voice cracked, "but without Mr. Weston around, the charges prolly won't stick."

"And the Reid civil suit?"

"I dunno. I didn't ask. Sounds bad, I know, but I was more worried about going to jail."

"Which you've luckily avoided."

"Look, I know what you're gettin' at, but you're forgetting somethin' important: how'd I know Mr. Weston was gonna be at your house?"

"I'm sure you have friends who still worked for Speedy Septic. Besides, Weston was driving one of those bright yellow well service trucks the day he died. It wouldn't be very difficult to follow him to our place."

"I didn't. I swear I didn't."

"Where were you yesterday?"

"Work."

"Where are you working?"

"Nowhere. No one will hire me with the truck thing hangin' over my head. I've been doin' odd jobs here and there."

"And yesterday?"

"I was up on the mountain cuttin' firewood for a friend."

"You were there all day?"

"'Til it started raining. Then I packed up and came home."

"And this friend can vouch that you were there?"

"Yup. I'll give you his number if you want."

"Save it for the cops. They'll want to speak to the person who can give you an alibi for the day. This friend was with you the entire time you were there, right?"

Middleton's face grew red. "N-no... he was at work all day. That's why he had me cut the firewood. He ain't got the time to do it himself."

Nick frowned. "Hmm."

"Look, I know what you're thinking, and I ain't no murderer!" Middleton rose to his feet again. "If you're looking to hang someone, check out ol' man Reid. When I got arrested, he lost his best chance at getting even with Mr. Weston. If that ain't motive, I don't know what is."

Amidst the barks of Luke, Josh Middleton stormed into the trailer and slammed the aluminum screen door behind him.

Chapter

NICK DROVE OUT of the Wiley Campgrounds and back over the railroad tracks into Teignmouth proper. There, the reemergence of the sun combined with the now-milder temperatures had inspired legions of tourists, shopping bags in hand, to take to the town on foot.

"My god, look at them all," Stella exclaimed as the Smart car inched along Main Street. "It's like being at Loehmann's during tax-free week."

"Mills and Alma warned us that today would be busy."

"This traffic is almost enough to make me wonder if it's worth running around town questioning people."

Nick looked over in surprise.

"I said *almost*. We learned too much this morning to make me think otherwise."

"Yeah, we did. Namely, that Josh Middleton probably won't be inviting us to his next Super Bowl party. Oh, and I wouldn't expect a Christmas card from him either."

"You can't blame him, Nick. The kid made one mistake in his young life and now he's expected to take the rap for everything from floating septic tanks to stolen trucks. Then, today, we walk in and suggest he might be involved in murder. It must be frustrating for him."

"Yes, it would be, assuming he's innocent. But what if he isn't? What if he killed Weston?"

"Then we've probably ticked him off enough to become his next victims," she joked. "Seriously, though, if his story is accurate, I don't see how he could have done it. By the time he would have finished chopping wood, Weston had bled to death, and we were already at the house."

"You're assuming a lot, don't you think?" asked Nick.

"I know, we have no proof that he was there all day. His friend might not be able to substantiate his story, but maybe someone else saw him. Someone should look into it."

"Unless someone watched him all day or remembers the exact time they spotted Middleton, it doesn't much matter."

"What do you mean it doesn't matter?" Stella said. "Middleton said he was chopping wood until it started raining. As long as someone saw him just before it started raining, he's in the clear."

"How do you figure that?"

"Because I clearly remember being in the living room of the farmhouse when the rain started coming down. It was about four thirty or so. By that time, Weston had long been dead."

"Yeah, I know. But you should also remember that Middleton wasn't working here in town."

"I know. He said he was working on the mountain. But I don't see how that changes anything," Stella said.

"Mountains tend to receive more precipitation and greater cloud cover than lower-lying areas. If Middleton was working at a higher elevation, he could have seen rain hours before we did. And if the mountain in question lies to the west of town, then he could have seen that front move through even earlier."

"Meaning he might have had ample time to shoot Weston and then return to the trailer park."

"Or wherever else he wanted to go."

"You know, you're kinda sexy when you talk like a park ranger."

"Just *kinda*?"

Stella laughed. "The only problem is Middleton didn't tell us which mountain he was working on."

"That shouldn't be too hard to find out. It sounded to me like 'on the mountain' is a phrase the locals use to mean a very specific area. We can ask Mills tonight or Alma tomorrah."

"Wow, you sound like a true Vermonter…"

"Yup. Pret' near."

"…who just came back from a trip to Jersey."

"Gee, thanks."

"Mmm. I'm a bit troubled by our visit with Alice, though."

"What about Alice?" Nick asked.

"Something about her timeline doesn't quite add up. If she left our house at a quarter after eleven, she should have had more than enough time to make the closing at noon, but instead she was late."

"She said she had phone calls to make."

"Okay, so she goes back to her office to make the phone calls and then walks a block to the lawyer's office where we met. I can buy that. However, what I can't buy is the fact that when Alice arrived, she was flustered and out of breath."

"Maybe the phone calls she made were with a difficult client."

"Or maybe she had been at the farmhouse the whole time. Maybe she stuck around to talk to Weston, and maybe that conversation turned ugly, and maybe she shot him."

"What motive did she have?" asked Nick.

"I don't know, but she was so adamant about never having done business with Weston. In the words of Shakespeare, 'the lady doth protest too much.'"

"You know, you're kinda sexy when you're quoting Shakespeare."

"I'm already sexy. I believe the word you're looking for is *sexier*."

Having coiled their way through the throng of cars and jaywalking pedestrians, Stella and Nick emerged at the opposite end of the village where, with the exception of the incredibly slow-moving tour bus in front of them, the road opened up, and the noise and congestion of town gradually dissipated.

Stella watched as Teignmouth's storefronts gave way to rolling farmland, acres of national forest, and, standing guard in the distance, the rounded, tree-covered peaks of Vermont's Green Mountains. It was here, in front of an expansive farmstand offering pumpkins, cornstalks, and cider doughnuts, where the bus finally pulled onto the shoulder of the road and joined other buses as they discharged a flock of tourists dressed in jeans, jackets, and sheepskin-lined boots. Some made a beeline for the doughnut stand, others headed directly for the pumpkin patch, and still others stood immediately outside the bus, snapping photos, typing messages onto tiny keypads, or shouting into cell phones.

Stella drew a heavy sigh and wondered if any of the motor coaches in the farm's gravel-lined lot had room for two more passengers. Although she and Nick had been in Vermont for just under twenty-four hours, she was already tired of the rural life. She missed the comfort of their Murray Hill apartment and the familiar sounds of car horns, traffic, and the occasional police or ambulance siren. However, she knew that she couldn't go back.

Whether it was the experience of finding a dead body in their well, sleeping in a hunting camp, or trying to realize her sleuthing skills, something had transpired to make Stella feel as though she were different from the urban sightseers who, despite having joined the leaf-peeping exodus, did their best to seem unimpressed by it. Not better than nor wiser than, mind you, just *different*.

No, Stella resolved, even if it didn't feel very welcoming at the moment, this place was her home now. And whatever Vermont living meant, she would do her best to embrace it.

While Stella grappled with the realities of her new environment, Nick longed to enjoy a driving experience seldom known to most city dwellers. Spying the freshly blacktopped, highly scenic, and completely open road that stretched before him, he passed the bus and quickly accelerated.

But, alas, before he could reach the 55-mile-per-hour speed limit, Nick spotted a sign indicating that the turnoff for Hank Reid's house lay just a few hundred feet ahead. Swearing under his breath, Nick veered onto the dirt and gravel of Deer Run Road and pulled into the driveway of the house designated as number 68.

Developed on generously subdivided farmland, the residences along Deer Run Road represented over one hundred years of architectural styles. Bungalows stood next to American Foursquares, Colonial revivals neighbored split levels, and ranches sprawled beside quaint cottages. Clad in white aluminum siding with turquoise trim and shutters, Hank Reid's mid-century undormered

Cape Cod not only bridged the gap between the centuries but served as a reminder of a simpler time in America's history.

With her hand on the wrought iron handrail, Stella climbed the brick front steps and pressed the doorbell. From inside, she heard the muffled sound of the Westminster chime.

"I'm going to let you do most of the talking with this one," Nick instructed. "Since you'll probably get further than I will."

"Why will I get further?"

"Uh, let's see. Tall, seemingly fast-talking Jersey guy or good-looking thirty-something blond with, let's face it, a nice rack. Gee, I wonder which of us the old guy would rather talk to?"

"You're a pig. We haven't even met this guy and you've already summed up that he's a dirty old man."

"Most of them are. You know why? Because they can get away with it. Even the most jealous guy on the planet isn't going to say anything to an old man who flirts with his girl, because once you do that, you look like an insecure jerk. The old guys know it too, 'cause they used to be us," Nick said, hiking a thumb at his chest. "They're crafty that way."

"You know, just when I start to think that perhaps men are deeper than we women give them credit for, you say or do some-thing to change my mind."

"Just keeping it real, babe. My perfection could cause you to have a distorted view of the male gender. As your husband, I feel it's my duty to demonstrate how other men might act. You know, just to remind you that you'd find most of them offensive."

"You're doing an awesome job, hon. A truly awesome job."

As Nick laughed, the front door swung open, revealing a balding, heavyset man in his seventies. "Yes?"

"Hi, Mr. Reid? I'm Stella Buckley, and this is my husband, Nick. We just bought the old Colton place."

Reid's round face broke into a wide smile. "Ohhh, yes. Come on in. I heard all about you folks when I was down at Alma's this morning. They failed to mention how pretty you were, though."

As Reid held the door ajar to allow Stella admittance, Nick turned on one heel as if to head back to the car. "Well, it looks like you have everything under control. I'll go get another flashlight and pick you up at—"

Before he could finish, Stella grabbed him by the arm and yanked him inside the house.

There, they encountered a tidy living room that might have doubled as the set of a 1950s television sitcom: the mint-green walls were offset by a white drop ceiling, the floor was covered with green tweed carpet squares, and the windows were dressed with metal Venetian blinds and stiff, floral-printed barkcloth drapes. Standing in the center of the room and in stark contrast to the softness of the carpet, seating, and drapes stood a teak coffee table with slender legs and rounded corners. A gooseneck metallic floor lamp with twin sconce shades cast a glow from its spot in the corner. Indeed, the room's only concession to the current age was a 42-inch LCD flat-screen television, and even that rested upon a Danish-modern maple credenza.

"Can I get you anything to drink?"

"No, thank you, Mr. Reid."

"I'll have a glass of water," Nick answered, although he might as well have been invisible.

"Please, call me Hank," the elderly man insisted as he sank into an angular club chair upholstered in green Optik fabric.

"Hank," Stella repeated as she sat down on a boxy, pinkish colored Herculon loveseat.

Nick selected the seat beside his wife but, finding the loveseat's small scale somewhat prohibitive, opted to perch tentatively on the edge of the sofa cushion.

"So, Stella—" Reid started. "That is what you said your name was, wasn't it?"

"Yes, Stella. Stella Thornton Buckley."

"Stella," Reid smiled. "That means 'star,' you know. And I'm sure a girl as pretty as you are has been the star of many a young man's eye."

"Here we go," Nick said under his breath.

The smile evaporated from Reid's face. "And what was your name again, young man?" he asked rather curtly.

"Nick, sir. Nick Buckley."

"Dick?"

"No, Nick," he corrected, taking great pains to enunciate the letter N.

"Huh? Rick?"

"Nick," he said even louder. "With an *N*."

"Mick?"

"No, Nick."

"Yeah, Dick. That's what I said the first time."

Stella had heard enough of the ridiculous exchange. "Mr. Reid," she interrupted. "Er, Hank—we'd like to ask you about Allen Weston."

"Don't know what I can tell you 'bout him 'part from the fact he's dead. Good riddance, I say."

"His death is precisely why we're here. You see, Allen Weston didn't fall down the well by accident; he was shot."

Reid, just like Alice and Josh before him, remained calm.

"Oh yeah? High time he got what he deserved."

"What did he do to you to merit such contempt?"

"You mean you haven't heard I was suing him?" He chuckled. "People 'round here ain't what they used to be if that story hasn't reached your ears yet."

"I heard snippets of the story but not all the details. Besides, I only trust half of what I hear as gossip. When I'm looking for the truth, it's best to go straight to the source."

"You're as smart as you are pretty," Reid complimented before recounting the tale of the floating septic tank. Not surprisingly, his story matched Josh Middleton's almost exactly.

"So how did you get everything fixed?" Stella asked at the end of his narrative.

"Wound up calling Jake Brunelle. Should have called him from the get-go, but I was afraid he'd take too long. Hired him to build me a shed once, and I swear the blackbirds might have turned white by the time he finished. A man can live awhile without a shed, but he can't live long without a ..." He threw his hands in the air, as if the gesture somehow signified the unmentionable piece of plumbing.

"No, I suppose he can't, can he?"

"When I saw the ad for Speedy Septic in the *Pennysaver*, I said, 'That's the ticket. That's what I need: speedy.' Well, they were fast, all right. Weren't here more than fifteen minutes before my septic system was screwed up. Awfully fast in leaving, too, though at least the one fella, Middleton, apologized before he left."

"Did Middleton explain what had happened?"

"No. He was pretty worked up about the situation. All he could say was 'I'm sorry about this, sir.' But I heard him on the phone talking to his boss, Weston—or, more precisely, I overheard how Weston was talking to him. Tough not to, the way he was hollering and carrying on."

"When did Middleton finally tell you that Weston had pushed to complete your job?"

"It was a few weeks later. Jake had just finished repairing the connections and setting in the new tank when Middleton showed up on my lawn, looking mighty sheepish."

"Middleton came here?" Nick clarified.

"Yup. Found out why he looked so sheepish, too. You know, Weston actually had the audacity to send him with a bill?"

"Weston billed you? For what?"

"Parts and labor. He wanted me to pay seventy-five dollars for each of the guys he sent here. One hundred and fifty dollars for less than a half hour of work! Can you believe it? And not only did I not get a new tank, but you know damned well he turned around and sold it to someone else."

"And he didn't send an apology? Didn't call?"

"Hell, no. Just a big fat bill! I tell ya, that's what's wrong with this country today. No one wants to take responsibility for anything. They overpromise, underdeliver, and then, when something goes wrong, it's the customer's fault."

"Was that the straw that broke the proverbial camel's back? Is that when you decided to sue Weston?" Stella presumed.

"Sue him? I wanted to destroy him. Oh boy, was I mad!" Reid pointed behind his chair. "Took every ounce of willpower not to grab one of those, drive to Weston's office, and put him out of his misery."

Stella stood up to see where the elderly man was pointing. There, obscured from the sofa by the angular club chair, sat a glass-enclosed case containing seven rifles of varying lengths and gauges. Despite Hank Reid's assertion that he had resisted temptation, she couldn't help but wonder if one of those rifles could have discharged the bullets that killed Weston.

Nick crossed the room to admire the cabinet and its contents. "That's quite the collection. Are you a big hunter?"

"Sure am. Don't go as much as I used to—the cold and damp bothers my arthritis somethin' fierce—but when the weather's mild and dry, there's nowhere I'd rather be. Say, if you like those, I should show you the den."

"There's more?"

"Oh yeah, another half dozen. And then there's my collection of handguns." He struggled to rise from his chair.

"Oh, I don't think Nick wants to see that right now," Stella suggested. "We'd like you to finish the story first. Maybe you can show Nick the den before we go."

Reid nodded in acquiescence and then told Nick excitedly, "It's not just guns back there. I have the antlers from the first buck I shot. Had them mounted. My wife, rest her soul, hated all that stuff. What you see here was all her doing. She tucked me away in a spare bedroom. Still, she was a good woman. I'll have to show you the rifle I used to win her with. It's hanging on the wall over my desk."

Nick's eyes narrowed. "Win her? What did you do, fight in a duel?"

"Pret' near. Emma was seeing some other fella when I met her. Dumb as a stump he was, too. So I invited him out hunting. I was a good shot back then; still am, but I pretended otherwise just to get his confidence up. Well," Reid started laughing, "I spent the whole morning missing everything I shot at. By the time the day was half-way through, that fella was feeling mighty superior. That's when I suggested we split up; he agreed because I was scaring away all the wildlife. Well, I let him get some ways ahead of me before I tracked him. Him being so dumb, it wasn't hard. I snuck up behind him and shot him in the shoulder."

"What? On purpose?"

"Yup. Told the game warden and the police that I mistook him for a turkey."

"And they believed you?"

"'Course. Damned fool didn't call out and tell me his where-abouts while he was moving, like you're supposed to. Far as any-one knew, I saw the moving brush and fired. Fella knew he had done wrong by not calling out, so he couldn't argue, but he didn't exactly believe me either. He called it off with Emma a few days later." Reid's eyes sparkled. "I think he figured out not to mess with ol' Hank Reid."

"I'm surprised you didn't take Allen Weston out hunting," Stella commented.

"I admit the idea did cross my mind," Reid laughed. "But I'm not quite the hothead I used to be. Weston wouldn't have gone hunting anyways. He was too much of a pantywaist flatlander for that."

"So instead of taking Weston out hunting, you opted to sue him."

"I had already seen a lawyer when Middleton showed up at my door, but I was advised to try and settle the whole thing out of court. I had half a mind to follow that advice until I looked at the bill Weston had sent along. When Middleton saw how angry I was about it, he told me what really happened that day. He told me how he had warned Weston about the flooding in my yard and how Weston had disregarded his warnings. I had suspected as much after hearing parts of their phone conversation, but Middleton confirmed everything. What's more, he agreed to tell his story in court, which was like winning the lottery. You see, without evidence, a jury might assume that Weston didn't know of the risks of digging up the old tank."

"And Josh Middleton provided that evidence," Nick concluded.

"Right. Before Middleton came forward, the most I could hope to gain from my lawsuit was reimbursement for my deposit. But with Middleton's testimony, I could take Weston to the cleaners for negligence."

"Until Middleton was arrested for stealing Weston's truck," Stella pointed out.

Reid grunted. "Talk about a waste of taxpayers' money. If the police had any smarts, they would have seen that for what it was: nonsense. Complete and utter nonsense."

"So you don't believe Middleton's guilty either."

"Hell, no. That young fella has more smarts and savvy than most people twice his age. Reminds me of myself when I was a kid in the army. Want to see the pictures of me in my uniform?" Reid asked Stella as he once again struggled to get out of his chair. "I served in Korea from 1951 to 1953—"

"In a bit." Stella motioned for Reid to sit back in his chair. "We were talking about Middleton's arrest."

"Oh, right, that." He shook his head in disgust. "It's obvious Weston got wind of Middleton's testimony and decided to put an end to it."

"Did he succeed? I mean, what did your lawyer say about Middleton's testimony, given the theft charges?"

"That if Middleton was in jail when my case went to trial, he prolly wouldn't be allowed to testify."

"And if he weren't in jail?"

"That anything he had to say would be pretty much useless anyway. The jury would think he had an axe to grind with Weston and authority in general."

"And now that Weston's dead?" Nick probed.

"Weston's insurance company would most likely settle for all damages. My deposit, the bill with Jake Brunelle—all of it would be paid for."

"Sounds like the answer to your prayers."

"You just wait a second there, Dick."

"Nick."

"I'm not so old that I can't tell what you're getting at!"

"He's not getting at anything," Stella interjected. "Except that you're lucky things turned out like they did."

"That's right," Nick agreed. "I'm more interested in your rifle collection than this whole Weston business. Did you happen to go out hunting yesterday?"

"'Course I did—at least 'til it started raining. I told you 'bout my arthritis. But I don't let it stop me. That's what fall is all about: hunting. Isn't it, Dick?"

"Nick. Did you get any bear?"

"Nope. Didn't hit a thing."

"Really? I thought you were a good shot."

"I am, but even good shots can have an off day."

"So you didn't shoot anything? Not even accidentally?"

"Now look here, Dick. I did not shoot Allen Weston. Am I glad that he's dead? Hell, yes. He was a perfect example of what's wrong with America today. Greedy, liberal slimeball. Good riddance, I say. Good riddance!"

Seeing their cue to exit, Stella rose from the loveseat. "I'm sure Dick—"

"Nick."

"—didn't mean anything by his comment. He was simply trying to scare up a good hunting story."

"Well, if that's the case, why didn't you just say so? I have tons of stories."

"Oh, and I know he'd just love to hear them. Unfortunately, however, we're out of time for today. Thank you for a lovely visit, Mr. Reid—um, Hank."

Reid, having previously struggled to rise to his feet, was out of his chair like a shot. "Oh, you're going? So soon?"

"I'm afraid so."

"Yeah, we have some things to take care of." Nick stood up and extended his hand.

"But you didn't see the den or my war pictures," Reid whined as he shook the younger man's hand.

"How about a rain check?" Stella suggested with a brilliant smile.

"You got a date. Oh hey, just one more thing. If you two are trying to play detective, you'd best be careful. I'm a pussycat, but not everyone in town is as nice as me. I'm also not the only one who might have gained from Weston being six feet under."

Stella struggled to hide her surprise at Reid's use of the word *pussycat*. "Um, really?"

"Yep. The kid, Middleton—as much as I like him, I bet it'll be hard to make those charges stick now that Weston's gone. And Jake Brunelle? He had to close shop all winter because Weston was taking away all his business."

"Hmmm. We'll be certain to check that out," Stella assured him as she inched closer to the front door.

"Hmph," Reid grunted in approval. "You do that. And watch yourselves. This might be a small town, but it's chock-full of nuts."

Chapter 9

THE WINDSOR BAR and Grill was housed in a circa 1700 tavern set back from the main road just on the edge of town. Its generic white clapboard exterior, faded carved wooden sign, and unpaved parking lot presented a forbidding façade to passing tourists, but the locals knew that inside they would be met with cozy stone fireplaces, coffered ceilings, and some of the best comfort food in town.

"My money's on Dick Cheney," Nick asserted as he slid into a corner booth.

"Who?" Stella asked from across the table.

"Hank Reid and that whole shooting accident story? He practically told us how he did it *and* how he plans to get away with it."

"By saying he mistook Weston for a turkey? Even if he shot Weston, I doubt he'd use that old story again."

"I don't know," Nick said. "If he can shoot a friend and lie his way out of getting caught, he could easily do the same with Weston."

"It wasn't his friend. It was the boyfriend of the girl he wanted to date. Guys that age do some pretty stupid things to impress a girl."

"Yeah, but shooting someone?"

"You're right. It does sound a bit extreme, doesn't it?"

"A bit?"

"Okay, so Reid's a loose cannon," Stella admitted, "but you're forgetting something: it was damp and cool when Weston was killed. Would Reid have been able to pull off an accurate shot, what with his arthritis acting up?"

"Oh, come on. You don't actually believe that whole rheumatism tripe, do you? Did you see him when we told him we were leaving? He couldn't have moved any faster if we had told him there was an all-you-can-eat buffet down the road."

"You're terrible, you know that?" she chided with a suppressed grin.

"I'm not terrible, I'm honest. I don't buy the feeble old man routine for a second. If Reid's arthritis is as bad as he claims, he wouldn't have been out hunting in the cold and damp yesterday. He would have been at home in his 1950s Barcalounger, sucking back a six-pack of Schlitz or Rheingold or whatever they drank back then and fantasizing about Laura Petrie in capri pants. I don't think Hank Reid's as frail as he makes himself out to be. He shot his wife's ex-boyfriend. He was in Korea for two years. He has antlers mounted in his den and a collection of firearms that rivals that of *Walker, Texas Ranger*. The dude's hard-core."

"That's just the generation, Nick. They're tougher than we are."

"There's tough and then there's trigger-happy. Look at my dad. He's only a few years younger than Reid, and you don't hear him rambling on about slimeballs who deserve to be shot—then again, maybe he did say something like that once. But it was years ago, on Christmas Eve, after a couple of Tom and Jerrys. And, to be honest, Uncle Dan always was kinda sleazy."

Their conversation was interrupted by the arrival of a brunette waitress dressed in a light blue Windsor Bar and Grill T-shirt, a faded pair of jeans, and a black half-apron. "You here for the burger special?"

"Yes," Nick replied.

"How you want them done?"

"Medium rare, please."

"Medium," Stella ordered.

"You want cheese? It's an extra fifty cents."

"Sure, I'll have cheddar."

"We don't have cheddar. All we've got is American."

We're in Vermont and you don't have cheddar? Stella thought to herself. "Um, that's okay. I'll pass."

"I'll pass too."

"Drinks?"

"Oh, it's been an interesting past two days," Stella prefaced. "I think I'll treat myself to a Cosmopolitan."

The waitress stared blankly.

Nick gestured at their surroundings. Along with the roaring fire, hanging lamps and a few neon beer signs cast a cozy glow over the dining room full of working-class couples and families. At the bar, about a half-dozen men in flannel shirts and hunting garb quietly drank their beer and exchanged stories of their latest kill. "I don't think this place goes in for the fancy mixed drinks, honey."

"Oops, sorry! I'll have a glass of wine, then. Do you have a pinot noir?"

"Nope," the waitress stated flatly. "We have two things: soda and beer."

"Really?" Stella uttered in disbelief.

"Just bring us two bottles of Sam Adams," Nick interceded on his wife's behalf.

"Comin' right up." The waitress nodded in Nick's direction before turning on one heel and heading back behind the bar.

"So," Nick picked up their previous conversation, "if you don't think Reid murdered Weston, who did?"

"I never said that I didn't think Reid did it. I just think we have other equally viable suspects."

"Josh Middleton's definitely on the list. But who else?"

"Alice, of course," said Stella.

"Eh, I'm still not sure Alice makes the cut. Problem is, like I said before, she doesn't have a motive."

"No, not that we know of, but I'm sure she has one. The way she spoke about Weston's business dealings was …"

"As if she were bitter about something?" asked Nick.

"Yeah, exactly. She sounded bitter, but about what? And why wouldn't she tell us who had done business with Weston? Everyone in town seems to know what's going on with everyone else. Why bother trying to keep it a secret?"

"Because the person who did business with Weston was either close to Alice or Alice herself."

Stella nodded. "Then, like you said, there's Middleton. Aside from having a strong motive and a shaky alibi, his behavior today was rather odd."

"How so?"

"Well, for a kid who claims to have felt so sorry for Hank Reid, he sure was quick to point the finger at him."

"Yeah, he was, wasn't he?" said Nick.

"Mmm-hmm. I have to wonder, was it self-preservation that made him put us on Reid's trail, or something else?"

"By 'something else,' you mean like Middleton discovering that Reid was trained as a government assassin during the Cold War and has never been deprogrammed? Because, personally, that's the vibe I get off of Reid. Look at where he lives. The last time that house was decorated, school kids were being taught to duck and cover whenever they saw a flash."

Stella, ignoring her husband's silliness, went on. "Then there's Jake Brunelle..."

"Brunelle? Why is he on the list?"

"You heard Reid. Weston was ruining Brunelle's business."

"Yeah, but Mills spoke with him this morning at Alma's. Brunelle has an alibi."

"An alibi no one has looked into yet. Besides, Mills didn't even have the coroner's report when he spoke to Brunelle. We can hardly say he's exonerated."

Nick shrugged. "Mills seemed satisfied with Brunelle's response. The two of them are even going hunting next weekend."

"I know he's the sheriff, but until we know more about Mills, I'm not going to take that as a ringing endorsement. You know how small towns are."

"Wow, cynical much? You're starting to sound like me," Nick said.

"No, I'm not. I'm not saying I think Mills is corrupt. I just think that in a small town where everyone knows each other, it would be difficult to retain a sense of objectivity. If Mills is friends with Jake Brunelle, it would be only natural that Mills would give him the benefit of the doubt."

"I don't know. Mills has been a cop for a while. If he had a problem putting his personal feeling aside in order to enforce the law, he'd have been out of a job a long time ago. If he seems satisfied with Brunelle's alibi, I trust his judgment."

"And I don't blame you for doing so, but I think we need to look at every possibility. Personally, I don't think we know Mills well enough to blindly follow his lead. I mean, he seems like a decent guy, but I'm not convinced he didn't have his own issues with Weston. That goes for Alma too."

"Yeah, I keep thinking about Alma's description of Weston this morning, and Mills's somewhat cryptic comment about him 'taking what he wanted.'"

"I know. Those were some cutting remarks to make about someone they claimed not to know very well."

"You think they know more about him than they let on?"

"I don't know. In a town this small, it's tough to tell. They could have had a run-in with Weston, they could be reacting to something they heard, or we could just be reading too much into it," she admitted. "However, I do think that if Alma was the one with the ax to grind, Mills would go to her defense in a heartbeat."

"Well, if he's trying to get into her—"

Stella shot him a warning glance. "Good graces? Please tell me you were going to say 'good graces.'"

"Um, if he's trying to hook up with Alma, rescuing her at her time of need would be the logical way to do it."

"It would. But, again, this is all conjecture. The only thing we know for certain is that Weston was shot and his body found stuck in our well."

"That's not all. We also know that Weston's truck was missing from the scene."

"You're right. That truck is a real puzzle. Why would it have been at the house while Alice was there in the morning and then disappear later in the day? And where is it now?"

"I have no idea," Nick gazed over Stella's head, toward the bar area. "But here comes Sheriff Mills. Maybe he has some news."

Mills, still in uniform, approached the table with a frosty glass mug in hand. "Evening. See you took my advice about burger night."

"We figured anyone who goes to Alma's every morning must appreciate good food."

Stella's mention of Alma's name caused the sheriff to clear his throat and stare uncomfortably at his shoes. "Well, it ain't a fancy place, but the people are friendly. Food's basic but good, and you get a lot of it."

"Yeah, it seems great," Nick remarked. "Hey, did you eat yet?"

"Nope, only just started to whet my whistle." Mills held his beer aloft with a grin.

"Then come and join us. We only just ordered, and we've yet to whet our whistles." Nick slid from his side of the booth and took a seat beside his wife.

"I don't want to intrude," Mills said slowly. However, his body language made it clear that he was happy for the invitation.

"You're not," Stella assured.

Mills slid into the spot recently vacated by Nick. "Thanks. Oh, and don't worry about the beer. Might be in uniform, but I'm off-duty."

"Whew! I know that's a load off *my* mind. The moment I saw you with that beer, I said to myself, 'Gee, I hope our law enforcement officers don't drink on the job.'"

Mills chuckled quietly and leaned across the table. "Between you and me, Mrs. Buckley, you might be better off if a few of them did."

As the trio laughed, the waitress returned with the Buckleys' beers.

"Oh, hey there, Suzanne," Mills addressed the waitress. "These folks are my guests tonight. Make sure everything goes on my tab, okay?"

"You got it," Suzanne replied over the Buckleys' protests. "Just promise me you won't chew their ears off or get too rowdy."

Mills blushed crimson. "Do my best."

"You didn't have to do that," Nick admonished.

"Yeah, I did. Least I can do for keeping you outta your home."

"That's not your fault. It's police business."

"I know. Can't help feeling kinda bad about it, though. I've been to Ray Johnson's camp before. Seen Sally Ann's with better furniture in them."

"It's not that bad. Still better than trying to sleep in the car."

"It would be better if we had our air mattress, though," Stella added.

"Funny you said that, Mrs. Buckley. After we left Alma's this morning, I gave a call over to Clyde Perkins. You can get one at his store."

"So, I finally get to meet this Clyde character. After everything I've heard, I feel as though I know him," Nick commented. "Where is Perkins, anyway?"

"Just down the street from here. Open 'til eight, so stop in after dinner."

"We'll do that. Maybe they have a flashlight too."

"What happened to your flashlight?"

"Long story," Stella sighed.

"Oh. So, um, what did you want to ask me?"

"Huh?"

"When I was on my way over here, I overheard you saying you needed to ask me something."

"Oh, I was wondering if you had any news on Weston."

"As a matter of fact, I do."

"Care to share with us?"

Mills drew a heavy sigh.

"Come on," Stella urged. "You know you can't keep it a secret from us; not in this town, anyway. If it doesn't wind up in tomorrow's paper, someone will eventually blab about it to us—it's inevitable."

"I got the coroner's report," Mills capitulated. "Weston was shot three times in the chest with a .30-06 hunting rifle."

"Does that mean you were right? That it was a hunting accident?"

Mills shook his head. "He was shot from a range of approximately forty to fifty feet. I drew a circle with a fifty-foot radius around your well, and it didn't even come close to making it to the woods. Nope, wherever the shooter was standing, he—or she—had to have seen Weston."

"So the shooter was standing somewhere in the yard or driveway."

"Or inside the house. Part of that circle goes right through your kitchen."

"Meaning that someone—someone who knew Weston would be working on our well—could have been inside the house, waiting. Waiting to kill him."

"That's right."

Stella envisioned a shadowy figure leaning out the kitchen window, hunting rifle cocked and at the ready. "Wait one minute; if someone shot him from *inside,* that means … oh, no. Don't tell me."

"Yup, it means that you probably won't be able to return to your house for quite a while."

"Is that why you checked on the air mattress for us?"

"Nope, that was just me being neighborly. Didn't get the coroner's report until long after I checked into Perkins, but it is why I'm buying dinner," he added with a quick grin.

"Three bullets at close range," Nick thought aloud. "No wonder there was so much blood."

"Weston bled out, all right, but not all that red water you saw was blood."

"What was it?"

"Neutrichrome red."

"Care to phrase that in non-Mr. Wizard terms?"

"Red fabric dye."

"So what? Weston was wearing a new shirt. How is that important?"

"Didn't say it was important. It might be, but it might not. Found it interesting, that's all."

"If Weston was shot at close range, does that mean he died fairly quickly?" Stella jumped in. "Because that would affect the time of death, right?"

Mills took a swig of beer and nodded. "Coroner puts Weston's death somewhere between ten AM and noon."

"Hmmm. And what about Weston's truck?"

"Oh, we found that this morning."

"Really? Where was it?"

"Couple of hikers found it parked on a trail in the woods 'bout an eighth of a mile behind your house. The keys were in the ignition."

"How strange."

"Most folks leave their keys in the ignition 'round here, but I agree with the spot being strange. A man working on your house would want his truck—and, most of all, his tools—nearby."

"Alice said that Weston's truck was at the house when she got there," Nick recounted. "Maybe that's when he unloaded his tools."

"Could be," Stella allowed. "She said he hadn't started work yet when she stopped by."

"Right. But does that mean Weston moved the truck after unloading it? I mean, why would he do that? It doesn't make any sense."

"Alice?" Mills asked, his face a question. "You talked to your real-estate agent today?"

"Y-yes," Stella stammered. "You know how you get a brief warranty time when you first move into a house? We wanted to see if we could get ours extended since we're not actually living there."

"And that somehow led to you telling her about the Weston case, did it?"

"Yes. How could it not? After all, that's what's preventing us from moving in."

"Doesn't mean you should have told her about the truck though, now, does it?"

Stella blushed bright scarlet.

"Oh, go on. You were saying that Alice saw Weston's truck at the house when she stopped by."

"That's right."

"What time was that?"

"Between ten thirty and eleven o'clock."

"Interesting."

The waitress interrupted briefly to deliver their food.

"It is interesting," Stella continued once the waitress was gone. "Especially given the time of death you just presented. The only thing we can't explain is what motive Alice Broadman would have for wanting Allen Weston dead."

"I've lived here my whole life, and I can't think of any. She didn't mention or hint at anything to you?"

Stella didn't want to put Sheriff Mills on Alice's trail until she had explored her suspicions. "No, not a word. But even if she had, it still wouldn't explain why Weston's truck was parked in the woods. Have you come up with any explanation for it?"

Mills lifted the bun from his burger and applied a generous dollop of ketchup. "I can think of a reason or two, but they're only guesses at this point."

"Care to share?"

"Sure would, but the State of Vermont wouldn't be too happy if I did. They're none too keen on us throwing around wild theories." Mills slid the ketchup bottle to Stella.

"No matter. We can probably figure it out." Stella poured the ketchup onto the side of her plate and passed the bottle along to Nick.

"We can? I'm not even sure I know where to begin," Nick said as he doused his burger and fries.

Mills chuckled and dove into his burger.

"At the beginning." Stella bisected her burger and dipped half of it in the ketchup. The sight of the oozing red substance triggered a question. "Sheriff Mills, you didn't mention it, but was there any blood in the truck?"

"Mrs. Buckley, I shouldn't … oh, hell. You'll just wheedle it out of someone else, won't you? No, there was no blood."

"Then we can rule out that Weston was shot there and his body moved to the well later."

"Hmm … you're pretty good at this. You a fan of those TV detective shows?"

"Not really. But my job in New York required analytical thinking at times."

"Oh yeah? What'd you do?"

Stella knew from experience that explaining the duties of a tapestry curator would either bore the sheriff or launch them onto another topic entirely. "I'll, um, I'll tell you some other time."

"So if there was no blood in the truck," Nick said between chews, "we can assume that Weston moved it there himself. Right?"

"Weston or his killer," said Mills. "The fact that it was found only an eighth of a mile away from the house would indicate that the driver wanted to hide that truck but still be within walking distance of the house."

"Okay, but why would his killer move it?" asked Nick.

"To buy some time," Stella guessed. "If we had pulled up and seen Weston's truck, we would have discovered his body much earlier than we did. Moving the truck to the woods—to where it couldn't be seen by someone approaching the house—would have ensured the killer a safe getaway. Now, if Weston moved it …" Stella took a bite of burger and pondered what possible reason a man would have to park his truck in the woods.

"Go on," Mills encouraged with a twinkle in his eye. "You've done a good job so far."

"Well, the only reason I can think of is that he was trying to hide from someone. But that doesn't make sense, does it? He was working outside for all the world to see."

"But he had access to your house, didn't he? And you can hear a car coming down your driveway before you even see it, can't you?"

"I don't know. I haven't been in the house long enough to test that."

It was a thinly veiled jibe, but Mills paid no attention. "So if Weston heard a car coming, all he'd have to do is go inside the house. Without his truck around, it would appear that he had left to go back to the shop or to get a bite to eat."

"I suppose. But how many people could have known he was going to be at our house?"

"I spoke to Weston's secretary about that. She said the only ones who knew he was working on your job were herself, Weston, Alice, and the two of you, of course. But when I was at the office, I noticed a schedule on the wall—a big, erasable whiteboard listing jobs, dates, and names of service people. Your job and Weston's name were on it. Anyone who came into the office could have seen it."

"The problem with that theory is our job was rescheduled from Wednesday, meaning that the correct date was only visible during the twelve to eighteen hours prior to the murder. That's a pretty tight window."

"Did Weston's secretary say why the appointment was changed?" Nick inquired.

"She had no idea why. Weston called her from his house Wednesday morning and simply said that it needed to be moved to the next day. Weston wasn't the type of man you questioned, so she kept her mouth shut and made the necessary changes. However, she did confirm Alma's statement about Weston never working on job sites. In the five years she's worked for the well company, yours is the first job he handled himself."

"That limits our suspects, doesn't it?" Stella noted. "If Weston never worked at job sites, the killer wouldn't think to look for his name on that board. That means the killer must have been told about Weston's movements by Weston's secretary or by Weston himself."

"Or they were a lucky son-of-a-so-and-so and just happened to spot Weston's name on the board while they were in the office."

"Yeah, but it's like we said to Alice this morning," Nick spoke up. "The well service trucks were bright yellow. You wouldn't need a military special-ops background to track the dude to our place."

"Those trucks are god-awful bright," Mills agreed. "You can see 'em for miles, even during a whiteout. Be easy to follow. Question is, who would do that? Sure, Weston ruffled a few feathers around town, but to lie in wait and then follow him—"

"Who said anything about lying in wait? The killer could have spotted Weston on the road, followed him to our house to talk to him, and things just got out of hand. It's hunting season. Riding around with a rifle in your vehicle wouldn't be unusual."

"As for who would do this—you're joking, right? I mean, as much as I hate to say it, Josh Middleton does have a motive, doesn't he?" Stella posed.

"Yeah. And what about Colonel Kurtz?"

Mills's eyes narrowed. "Who?"

"Hank Reid. Old guy. Big hunter. Uber-conservative. If he wasn't already bald, he'd still be sporting a flattop."

"I can see you two were busy today. You paid a visit to Middleton and Reid too, did you?"

Stella tried to deny it. "Ummm …"

Nick, however, came clean. "Yeah, we did. Middleton is your typical angry kid, but Reid is a total head case."

"Hank's an odd duck, at that."

"Odd? He shot his future wife's boyfriend in the shoulder."

"Told you that story, did he?" Mills chuckled.

"You're laughing. Does that mean it's not true?"

"Oh, it's true all right. Just laughing at how rattled you are by it."

"Yeah, well, call me a silly flatlander, but I'm not used to people using turkey hunting as a pretext to shooting each other."

"No different than city people claiming self-defense or insanity."

"Nope, it probably isn't. And once I shed my flatlander mindset, I'm sure I'll be as accustomed to it as you are, but for now, I find it a little bit unnerving."

"You can lose the mindset, but you'll never lose the name. Could live here the rest of your life, you'll still be a flatlander. Your children and your children's children too. Some say a family has to be here at least four generations 'til they're considered true Vermonters; some say more. It's open for debate."

"So we'll always be flatlanders like Weston."

"Yup. No one will call you that outright, of course, unless you tick 'em off. It's like Alma said. Weston didn't show respect. Came here, bought everything out, and aimed to build everything up. People here like things the way they are; they don't want a Walmart on the next corner. So long as you don't act as though you're better than most and try to change things, you'll do fine."

"We'd never do that," Stella assured.

Mills, having finished his meal, stood up and donned his hat. "That a fact? 'Cause changing things includes nosing around murder cases and possibly putting people in jail."

Stella blushed.

"I understand you're eager to get the bottom of this thing and move into that house of yours, but what you should be doing, Mrs. Buckley, is making friends. You need to convince folks you're one of them. Try dressing down a bit like the other ladies."

Stella surveyed her ensemble of dark indigo boot-cut jeans, black stiletto heel boots, and fitted V-neck knit top accessorized with a silk scarf, bangle bracelets, and a pair of silver hoop earrings in confusion. Was Mills suggesting she wear a hand-knit sweater? Or, worse yet, flannel?

"And get yourselves a truck. You need to fit in and blend—at least, that's what I'd be doing. Now, if you'll excuse me, I'd best be going. I have to get home and feed my cats. Mr. Roscoe and Mr. Rufus get ornery if they don't get dinner by nine o'clock."

As Mills walked to the bar to settle the tab, Nick turned to Stella. "Mr. Roscoe and Mr. Rufus? Oh yeah, he blends."

STELLA AND NICK left the Windsor Bar and Grill and drove the two blocks to the Perkins Family Store. Once inside, they realized that Perkins was not so much a convenience store as a purveyor of products guaranteed to satisfy every facet of Vermont country living. Shelves lined with patterned contact paper that would have seemed at home in Hank Reid's kitchen cabinets offered customers the usual suspects: breads, cereals, snacks, and an eclectic mix of canned and packaged foods. However, tucked alongside the pantry staples were such oddities as hand-carved turkey calls, bright orange rain ponchos, squirrel-proof bird feeders, home-baked organic dog treats, and souvenir bottles of maple syrup.

Lining the wall behind the cash register were the age-restricted items: rolls of lottery tickets, stacks of cigarette cartons, and boxes of ammo to fit nearly every caliber hunting rifle known to man. And, for those who would rather try their hand at catching (and then releasing) the local supply of brown, rainbow, brook, and lake trout—in addition to the typical eggs, milk, soda, and beer—glass refrigerator cases held plastic containers of nightcrawlers and other live bait. Alongside the cases, a display of nymphs, emergers, and buggers appealed to anglers.

Indeed, even the front porch of the store presented consumers with buying opportunities. Having been transformed into a seasonal outdoor supply section, the rickety floorboards were stocked with flower bulbs, rakes, locally grown pots of chrysanthemums, and bags of autumn fertilizer.

But possibly the most unique facets of the store were a back room filled to the rafters with the finest wines and spirits (including a few bottles of twenty-five-year-old Macallan Scotch priced at ninety dollars each) and a delicatessen counter whose blackboard listed the Hunter's Special of the Day as roasted turkey breast, arugula, and smoked mozzarella on rosemary and sun-dried tomato foccacia.

Doubtful that such a recipe would ever grace the pages of *Field & Stream* magazine, Stella could only assume that the Hunter's Special had been designed to please the thrill-seeking cliff-dwellers and suburbanites who arrived each autumn in their shiny Land Rovers with the latest L. L. Bean hunting gear.

As she and Nick perused the aisles for their bed, Stella found herself grinning at the idea of camo-clad grown men sitting cross-legged on red-and-white-checked blankets, sipping chardonnay, and nibbling, pinkies suspended in midair, on panini. When she imagined those same well-heeled Orvis-shopping sportsmen being forced to spend the night in Ray Johnson's hunting camp, she nearly laughed out loud.

Laughed out loud, that is, until she literally came face to face— or, more accurately, mouth to forehead—with a hobbitlike woman somewhere in her sixties. Standing just under five feet tall, she wore a pair of ill-fitting corduroy pants and a nubby, multicolored

Fair Isle sweater that only served to accentuate her saggy bosom. Her straight, slightly stringy, long white hair not only gave her the appearance of being quite ancient but failed to bring balance to a face permeated by an extremely large nose.

Stifling a scream, Stella reared back in surprise.

"Mrs. Buckley," the woman stated.

"Um, yes?" Stella replied, all the while wondering how this woman knew her name.

"I saw you with Alice today."

"Alice. Alice? Oh, you're the receptionist at the real-estate office! Yes... I knew that. It's just that seeing you with your hair down and so... so close up... threw me for a second there." Stella hoped that her "close up" comment would be a sufficient cue to make the woman step back a few paces. Instead, she leaned in closer.

"Mrs. Buckley, I need to talk to you."

"G-go ahead." Stella leaned back.

"In private."

"Um ... what—what's your name again?"

"Bunny."

Stella felt her mouth gape open. She had never before met anyone named Bunny, but if she had, this was not how she imagined the woman would have looked. "Um, Bunny, I—I don't think we need to go anywhere. You're close enough that no one else in the store could possibly hear you."

Again, Bunny missed her cue to back up. Glancing surreptitiously from side to side, she announced in a whisper, "Alice is lying."

"Lying about what? You listening at doors?" Stella replied in her normal speaking voice. "Don't worry about it. I never even gave it a second thought."

"Shh!" Bunny's eyes furtively danced about the store in search of an eavesdropper. "I mean she lied about Weston."

Stella lowered her voice. "What about him?"

"About doing business with him."

"Go on."

"There's a property down in Jersey. I'm not sure of all the details, but Alice invested in it. With Weston."

"The two of them? Together?"

Bunny nodded. "Lost money on the deal, too. Wasn't a problem for Weston, but for her …"

"How much?"

"I don't know the numbers, but I can tell you that she laid off the rest of the office as a result."

"I thought she did that because of the slow economy."

"There were two rounds of layoffs. The first one was because business had slowed down. That was just a few people, though. You know, the ones who were on salary but never earned a dime in commission. Got rid of the secretaries too. Trimming the fat, they call it. That's when she hired me."

"So you were there for the second layoff."

Bunny gave a single nod.

"And you saw papers stating that Alice and Weston were in business together."

This time, Bunny turned her head slowly from side to side. "No, I've looked, but I never found them."

"Then how do you know about this?"

The older woman arched an eyebrow. "How do you think?"

The corners of Stella's mouth turned up slightly. If Alice's statement about never doing business with Weston had been a lie, her assertion about Bunny listening at keyholes obviously wasn't. "What did you overhear?"

"Weston came to the office last week. Alice took him into the conference room and asked him for money."

"A loan?"

"No, more like paying her back. She told him he owed her for getting her into the mess she was in. Said she would never have gotten involved if he hadn't put up his money in the first place."

"Those were her exact words?"

"Not exact but pret' near."

"And how did Weston react?"

"He told her that she was a businesswoman and she should have known the risks before going into the deal. He then reminded her that he had lost money too. Alice didn't take to that very kindly. She went into a rage—yelling at him, swearing, you name it."

"Did she say anything specific during her outburst?"

"Yup. She said that she was still paying for her mistake."

"Still paying? What did she mean by that?"

"At the time, I figured she was being a drama queen. But a few days later, I went to pick up the office mail and saw a monthly statement from a mortgage company in Boston. It was addressed to Alice's home, but the post office had put it in the business box by mistake. Naturally, I peeked inside."

"Naturally."

"The address of the mortgaged property was in Hackensack, New Jersey, and the monthly payment was over $5,000."

"Do you still have the statement?"

"No. I sealed it back up and put it on Alice's desk. Why?"

"Because it would come in handy when you tell your story to the police."

"I'm not telling the police anything. I don't want to get Alice in trouble. I—I could lose my job."

Stella might have pointed out that the routine activities of listening through keyholes and opening the boss's mail were equally deserving of termination. However, given the crazed expression on Bunny's face, she decided that some subjects were best left unexplored. "Then why are you telling me about it?"

"I needed to tell someone. What if Alice killed that man? I couldn't let her get away with it."

"See? Generally, that's when most people would call the police with an anonymous tip."

"I didn't know it could be anonymous. And since you seemed to be nosing around—"

"I wasn't 'nosing.'"

"I thought I'd tell you what I knew and let you do what you want with the information."

"I see. So you don't want to get Alice in trouble, but you don't mind if *I* do." Stella's voice rose in annoyance.

"Shh!" Bunny looked around nervously. "No, that's not it at all. I just didn't know if it was important or not."

"Let's see. Alice was financially ruined because of a business deal she made with Weston. You didn't think that was important?"

"Of course I did. I'm telling you, aren't I? But … all right … I'll say it plain: if Alice killed Weston, who's to say she wouldn't do the same thing to me for ratting on her?"

"That's what you're really afraid of, isn't it? Be honest. You've worked for Alice for a little while. Do you think she could have shot Weston?"

"After hearing how angry she was, yes. Yes, I do."

"Then all the more reason for you to tell your story to the police. They can do a far better job at protecting you than I can."

"Protect me? Sheriff Mills?" Bunny scoffed. "Why, he'd be more apt to give the killer a big old pardon and a slap on the back for doing him a favor."

Stella's eyes opened wide. She knew there was a story behind Mills's comment that morning. "Why would Mills view Weston's death as a positive event?"

"'Cause of Alma, of course. Mills has been sweet on her for years. Whole town knows it. Heck, if you've been down to the Sweet Shop, you've probably seen it yourself."

"Yes, I noticed that he seems interested in her—romantically."

"Yeah, well, so was Weston."

"Weston and Alma?"

"Uh-huh. I'd seen Weston sniffing around Alma quite a few times in the past several months. Never saw him at her house—I live next door—so I can't say if there was something to it or not. And Alma's tightlipped when she wants to be, so I don't know if she returned the feelings, but if Mills noticed them flirting … well, let's just say that with Weston out of the way, he has a clear path to Alma."

"First it was Alice. Now you're trying to say that Sheriff Mills—"

"No! No, I'm not sure I'd go so far as to say that …"

"What are you saying, then?"

"Nothing. Nothing, except that some men will stop at nothing to impress a—" Bunny, her face registering a combination of shock and recollection, stopped what she was doing and stared at a spot somewhere above and past Stella's head.

Stella turned around but was unable to identify the cause of Bunny's sudden near-catatonic state. "What is it? What's wrong?"

"Nothing. I ... I, um ... I have to go."

"What? Now? But you were telling me—"

"There's nothing else to tell," Bunny snapped and rushed out of the store, bumping into Nick on the way.

"What's with Edna Winter? And where's she going in such a hurry?"

"That was Alice's receptionist. Her name's Bunny."

"Yeah, I know who she was. I was ju—" Nick began to explain before the meaning of his wife's words hit him. "Wait a minute, did you say Bunny? That woman was named *Bunny*?"

"I didn't believe it at first either."

"Yeah, wow. Either there was a point in her life when she was actually cute or the universe is playing a very cruel joke on her. Seriously, if all bunnies looked like that, no one would ever have put the words *Easter* or *Playboy* in front of them."

"Nick," Stella scolded.

"Sorry, it had to be said. She sure had your ear a long time, though. What did she want?"

"Lots of things. I'll tell you back at the camp." She nodded toward the stack of items Nick held in his arms. "Did you find everything?"

"Yeah. Some chocolate for my sweetie, a flashlight to replace the one you 'lost,' a bottle of wine to make up for yesterday's champagne," he said with a raise of his eyebrows, "and the air mattress."

"Oh, yes, the air mattress. Never in my life would I have imagined finding an inflatable bed so appealing."

"I probably liked them as a kid. But now?" Nick straightened his posture. "What do you say we get out of here?"

"I'd love it," Stella replied as she removed the chocolate bar from Nick's arms.

"Thanks, honey. That really lightened the load."

"Just doing my part." She followed him to the counter, where a somewhat elderly clerk was chitchatting with a woman who looked to be in her early forties.

The clerk gave Nick a brief glance before returning to his conversation.

The Buckleys waited in patient silence, but after several seconds had elapsed it became apparent that the clerk had no intention of ending his social hour prematurely. Was this the infamous Clyde that Alice had warned them about? Surely it must be, for Stella refused to believe that two men in the same town were capable of delivering such abysmal customer service.

Nick cleared his throat noisily.

The clerk showed no reaction.

"Did he hear you?" Stella whispered in her husband's ear.

Nick shrugged and then dumped his items beside the till. "Excuse me, sir."

The action brought about the desired effect. The clerk ceased talking and approached the cash register, but not before taking a long look out the store window at the Buckleys' vehicle. "Hmph," was his only remark upon seeing the license plate.

Nick's eyes slid to Stella, who was shaking her head in disbelief.

"I'm gonna need to see some ID," the clerk announced.

"For what?"

"The wine."

"I don't look over twenty-one to you?" Nick asked as he extracted his wallet from the back pocket of his jeans.

"Don't know what you look like. Only know I need a date for this here machine," he said, pointing to the cash register. "State law."

Nick flashed his wallet, which was opened to the clear plastic pocket that contained his New York State driver's license.

"Hmph," the clerk remarked as he peered over the top of his glasses. "You're the fella who bought the old Colton place, aren't you?"

"That's right."

If the Buckleys had anticipated the clerk's question to be a springboard for further discussion, they were sorely mistaken. Instead, he rang up the final item and silently hiked a thumb toward the total on the register to indicate that payment was due.

His wallet still in hand, Nick pulled out a dark blue debit card and searched the counter for the familiar keypad and card-swiping mechanism.

"We don't accept debit cards. Credit or cash only."

"I don't have cash."

The clerk pointed to the back of the store, where a bright red neon sign identified the gray mechanical device beneath it as an ATM.

Nick rolled his eyes at the blatant money-making scheme. "Can you run it as a credit card?"

"Won't post to your account 'til Monday."

"Yeah, that's okay."

"Suit yourself." The older man complied and, a few moments later, produced the same card, a pen, and a cash register receipt. The items on the counter remained loose beside the till.

"Do you think I could get a bag?" Nick asked as he signed the receipt.

The clerk heaved a heavy sigh, pulled a tall, thin brown paper bag from beneath the counter, and slid the wine bottle into it. Everything else he left.

"Gee, thanks. Thanks a lot," Nick said sarcastically. As he replaced his wallet in his back pocket and gathered up the air mattress and flashlight, Stella grabbed the wine and the chocolate and led the way to the shop door.

Once they and their purchases were safely ensconced in the Smart car, Nick looked at his wife and said, "You know, I can't wait to see Crazy Maggie again."

"Really? Why?"

Nick looked over his shoulder and backed out of the Perkins parking lot. "Because after meeting some of the yahoos in this town, I can't help but wonder how Maggie got the crazy label and no one else did."

"Hey, at least you didn't have Barbara Bush's ugly stepsister giving you the hairy eyeball."

"Yeah, really—what was that all about, anyway?"

Stella recounted Bunny's allegations against Alice. By the time she finished, they had arrived back at camp. Nick stepped from behind the driver's wheel and removed the air mattress and flashlight from the back hatch. "Do you think Bunny's telling the truth?"

Stella grabbed the wine; the chocolate bar had already made its way into her oversized leather handbag. "Yeah, I do, actually. She might have exaggerated a few of the details, but, fundamentally, I think her story's accurate."

"You're positive she's not just trying to get her boss into trouble? Because it seems strange to me that she'd tell *you* all of this and not the police."

"It seemed strange to me too. So I asked her."

With the car's headlights shining upon the front of the camp, Nick opened the front door, placed the air mattress and flashlight on the kitchen table, and proceeded to light the gas lamps. "And?"

"Well, there are two things standing in her way. First, she's afraid that she'll lose her job."

"She could give the police an anonymous tip."

"Second, she's afraid Alice will come after her next."

"Again, an anonymous tip would solve that problem. Likewise, I hope you explained that if Alice is the killer, we're all safer with her behind bars. Even if it got to the point where Bunny needed to testify in court, the police would make sure she was protected."

Stella threw her bag on the sofabed, placed the wine on the coffee table, and kicked off her high-heeled boots. "That leads us to the second part of the conversation. Apparently Bunny doesn't trust Sheriff Mills. It seems Weston had been frequenting the Sweet Shop as of late and apparently had his eye on Alma."

"So our hunch about their comments this morning was right: they *did* know Weston better than they let on. Well, at least Alma did, but that puts Mills in the role of the jealous..." Nick struggled to find the right word.

"Stalker?"

"I was going to go with admirer, but I guess a guy who clogs his arteries with jelly doughnuts every morning just to see a woman he never asks on a date could qualify as a stalker too."

"Ya think?"

"Does Bunny suspect Mills of pulling a Hank Reid?"

"A what? Oh, shooting the boyfriend," she shook her head and laughed. "She seemed undecided about that. At first she leaned toward no, but then she saw something that—"

"Changed her mind?"

"No, something that freaked her out."

"What did she see?"

"I have no idea. That's when she ran out of the store and headlong into you."

"Think it had something to do with Mills?"

"Your guess is as good as mine. All I can say with any degree of certainty is that although Bunny may be wary of Mills, she's definitely frightened of Alice. When I asked her if she thought Alice could be the killer, she replied with a definite yes."

"How about you? Do you think Alice murdered Weston?"

"I think it's completely possible. In addition to having a strong motive, Alice knew that Weston would be working on our well yesterday. And she was actually at the house around the time Weston was shot."

Nick nodded and then zipped outside. He returned several seconds later with his car keys in hand. "The thing that bothers me is, for some reason, I can't imagine Alice using a hunting rifle."

Stella flopped onto the sofa and pulled her cross-stitch supplies out of her handbag. "Why not?"

"First off, where would she have gotten it from? It's not like she has a gun rack in her car." He took a multifunction knife from his pocket, extracted the corkscrew tool, and set to work opening the wine.

"No, but if she knew Weston was going to be at our house, she could easily have taken a rifle from the house and put it in the trunk. Who knows? It's hunting season. She or her husband might have had one in the trunk anyway."

Nick popped the cork. "Okay, so we'll assume Alice had the rifle. She goes to the farmhouse, gets into it with Weston, and *bang*, she shoots him. What about the recoil? Alice is shorter than you and doesn't appear to be in very good shape. I doubt she has tremendous upper body strength. Few women do."

Stella started stitching the letter *E* on a blank piece of ivory Aida cloth. "What's your point?"

"The point is that a hunting rifle can have a powerful recoil—powerful enough to injure a shoulder if you're not careful or not used to firing rifles." He retrieved two mismatched juice glasses from the kitchen cupboard. "Alice didn't seem to be in pain when we saw her."

"For all we know, Alice goes hunting with her husband all the time. I'm sure lots of women around here do."

"Yeah, but she'd still be sore."

"A sore shoulder is easy enough to hide, Nick. It's not like a leg injury, which would cause a limp."

Nick nodded and filled each glass with wine. "True enough. Still, it will be interesting to hear her side of things. You know, when the police talk to her."

Stella stitched another letter *E* three spaces to the right of the first one. "I'm not telling the police anything yet."

"What? Why? She could be the murderer."

"She very well could be, but she could also be innocent. I'm not sending the authorities breathing down Alice's neck based on the story of some wire-haired woman we don't even know. Although we may not be close personal friends, we've known Alice for six months now. I think we owe it to her to let her tell us her side of the story before we go calling the cops."

Nick placed the glasses of wine on the coffee table. "I suppose. I just hope we're not getting in over our heads. I know you feel you have something to prove, but this is serious business, Stella."

Stella put down her cross-stitch piece and grabbed her glass of wine. "I realize that, but we're already involved, Nick. I don't see any other option but to move forward with our own investigation, particularly if Mills has a personal interest in keeping the identity of Weston's killer under wraps."

"You mean if Mills murdered Weston."

"Or if Alma did. It was apparent from Alma's comment that Weston had done something to hurt her. If Mills is protecting himself or her, this case could be open for a very long time."

Nick sat beside his wife. "Jeez, I didn't even think of that. We could be out of our house for months."

"Not only that, but who would bring Mills and/or Alma to justice?"

"Someone would have to report their suspicions to Mills's superior."

"Exactly," said Stella. "In order to do that, someone has to get to the bottom of things first. That someone is us."

"And to think just last week we were complaining about the stress of moving and buying a house. That seems like a cakewalk compared to this."

"I know. But if we devise a plan of attack, we should be able to put things together fairly quickly. Tomorrow, we start at the beginning of the alphabet, namely *A* as in Alice and Alma."

"Alma? You're not talking to Mills first?" Nick asked.

"Why would I? Given his remark this morning, it's clear he knew something was going on between Alma and Weston. I want to know what that something was."

"Probably just a fling, because unless there's a side to Alma I'm just not seeing, I can't imagine why she'd go for a guy like Weston."

"Maybe Weston was a different person around Alma. Maybe she brought out the best in Weston, kind of the way I do for you."

Nick clinked his glass against hers. "I think you have that the wrong way around. If anyone brings out the best in anyone—" he finished the statement by pointing to himself and then his wife.

"Dream on," she teased and then took a sip of wine. "Mmm, speaking of dreaming, shouldn't you start blowing up the air mattress?"

Nick swallowed a mouthful of wine and chuckled. "I'm not using lung power, you know."

"I know that. But it takes a little while, doesn't it?"

"Nope," he stood up and walked over to the kitchen table, where he had placed the folded mattress minutes earlier. "I got the mattress that comes with an air pump. Once we plug that baby in, it'll only take a ..." his voice trailed off.

Stella stood up and joined him. "What? What's the matter?"

"The pump is electric. We don't have electricity."

"Oh, no. Isn't there some other way to power the pump?"

"Sorry. I'm afraid I left my pocket generator in my other pair of pants."

"What about the car cigarette lighter?"

"Only if you want to set it on fire. I don't have a converter."

"So it's ..." She sighed and flopped back onto the sofa.

Nick flopped beside her. "Yep. Another night in the Slinky factory."

Chapter

11

STELLA AWOKE TO the sound of the camp door slamming shut, followed by the intoxicating aroma of freshly brewed coffee. She opened her eyes to see Nick perched on the edge of the sofabed, a white paper bag in one hand and a disposable cardboard tray bearing two coffee cups in the other.

He leaned over and kissed her bare shoulder and then her lips. "Morning."

Stella smiled and stretched. "Good morning. What's all that?"

"Alma's to go."

"Wow, you've been busy. What time is it?"

"Eight thirty. I got up and couldn't go back to sleep."

"I can't believe I didn't hear you." Stella sat up and immediately felt an intense ache in her right shoulder. She grabbed at it with her left hand. "Owwww."

"Yeah, that's exactly why I didn't go back to bed this morning. Felt like I slept on a picket fence. It gets better as you move around, though. Until then, I have just the thing to ease the pain."

Shaking the white bakery bag as he went, Nick walked toward the front door.

Mimicking a hungry dog, Stella threw back the blankets and swung her legs over the side of the inch-thick mattress. After donning a pair of plush mule slippers, she stood up and reached for an oversized hooded sweatshirt.

"You won't need that," Nick informed her as he juggled the white bag between his fingers and turned the front doorknob.

Stella obediently dropped her sweatshirt and, despite her rather scanty ensemble of boxer shorts and tank top, followed her husband outdoors.

As she stepped into the summerlike air, Stella at once understood that Nick's promise to ease the pain extended beyond mere coffee and baked goods to the scenery they were to enjoy while consuming them. Beyond the front porch and the skinning table, the patchy front lawn gave way to acres of deciduous trees in a sun-kissed palette of gold, scarlet, and ginger set against the cool azure of the cloudless sky and the dark purple of the distant mountains. It was a view so vibrant, so awe-inspiring, that upon gazing at it, one's troubles seemed to melt away.

"My god, it's beautiful."

Nick stood behind Stella and slid an arm around her waist. "So are you."

As they watched the woods in contented silence, Stella reached up and rubbed the side of Nick's face with her hand. This was the reason she had been looking forward to their move for so long. This wasn't just an opportunity for Nick to live out a lifelong dream, it was a chance for both of them to shake off the stress, traffic, and hustle and bustle of city life and learn to appreciate the peace, quiet, and simpler things in life. "You know, we've been so preoccupied lately that I almost forgot that this was here, right outside our front door."

"And, once this whole murder thing blows over, we'll get to enjoy it every day for the rest of our lives. Not this view, of course, but the one from the farmhouse isn't half bad either."

"It'll do. It's not quite Mr. Yang's chrysanthemum display, mind you, but I think I can learn to love it." She kissed him and then sat down in one of the unfinished Adirondack chairs.

"Would this help to win you over?" Nick stuck his hand into the white bag and produced a croissant slathered with raspberry preserves.

"Okay, now you're just showing off." She took a bite and immediately began to moan. "Mmm, yeah, another one of these tomorrow morning and I might just forget about that outhouse."

"Doesn't make up for that bed, though," he complained as he passed his wife a cup of coffee.

"Bed? I thought it was a torture device."

"No kidding. All night I kept kicking myself about that pump." He unwrapped the paper from a roll laden with a combination of egg, onion, and red pepper.

"Not your fault. We're used to living in the electrified age."

"When I was at Alma's, I asked Mills if he knew a place that sold AC car adapters."

"Any luck?"

"Nope, no dice. He suggested we try Rutland, but I know you have other things on the agenda than driving for three hours."

"Yeah, but if we need the adapter ..."

"No, I'll see if someone around here has one we can borrow."

"You didn't mention anything to Mills about Bunny stopping me last night, did you?"

Nick swallowed a bit of his breakfast sandwich. "He already knew. Seems the guy at the counter was Clyde Perkins."

"I kinda figured that by the way he was gossiping instead of working."

"Well, he stayed true to form. As soon as we left, he got Mills on the horn and told him that (a) we had bought the air mattress, and (b) Bunny had been chewing your ear off."

"Are you kidding me? Oh, I don't think I'll ever get used to this small-town mentality."

"Don't worry. He didn't know what Bunny talked to you about, and I sure didn't tell him. But even if I had, Mills seems to have branded her as an eccentric, so I doubt he would have believed me anyway."

Stella took a sip of coffee. "What about Alma and Weston? I hope that's still a secret."

"My lips are sealed. But you want to hear something funny? The minute Mills started talking to me about Bunny, Alma interrupted us to say she was coming by the camp tonight to bring us dinner."

"You think she was prompted by your conversation?"

"Almost positive. Why would she interrupt us to tell me that? Why not just wait until I was ready to go?" He took a large bite of the sandwich and then washed it down with a generous swig of coffee.

Stella, meanwhile, picked pensively at her croissant. "Did she happen to invite Sheriff Mills to join us?"

"Nope. She said she'd be here at six o'clock with dinner for the three of us."

"Hmmm. Not only didn't she invite the sheriff, but she made certain he understood that it was dinner for three. Do you think she might want to talk to us alone?"

"You're a woman—you'd know better than I would. I have a tough enough time figuring you out."

Grinning ear to ear, she leaned back in her chair and pulled her knees to her chest. "You do all right."

"Meh … oh, hey, speaking of doing *all right*, I got hit on this morning."

"Nick," Stella sighed, "you always think you're getting hit on."

"No, I always *say* I get hit on, but I don't actually believe it. This time I mean it, though. And guess who was doing the hitting."

"I don't know. Alma?"

"In front of Sheriff Mills? That's cold."

"Then I don't know. Who?"

"Betsy Brunelle."

"In front of her husband, Jake? Now *that's* cold."

"No, she was there by herself. I was standing by the counter, talking to Mills, waiting for Alma to fill our order, when in comes Betsy. She was in a hurry, kinda flustered. She gives a quick wave to Mills and then immediately walks right into me."

"And, naturally, that means she wants to sleep with you."

"Will you let me finish? After she bumps into me, she grabs my arm and apologizes, only she doesn't let go right away. Instead she moves her hand down my arm, all slow and soft and sexy like, and lets her hand linger on mine before she finally turns away to order her coffee."

"Seriously?"

"Seriously."

Stella was silent for a few moments. "Are you sure you're not exaggerating this?"

"No, I'm not exaggerating. I'm a grown man. I should know by now when a woman has the hots for me."

"Yeah, but you could have misinterpreted it. You said she was flustered. Maybe she was having a rough morning and bumping into you made her realize she needed to slow down, so she did."

"Why do you find it so hard to believe that Betsy Brunelle was hitting on me?"

"I don't. After meeting Jake yesterday, it makes perfect sense that she'd find you attractive. Not that you're unattractive, of course—on the contrary—but compared to Jake Brunelle ... well, that's like comparing me to Bunny."

"So she was coming on to me because her husband looks like Gimli from *Lord of the Rings*. Is that what you think?"

"No ... .well, maybe a little ... um, I'm thinking it was probably part Gimli and part vulnerability."

"Uh-huh. Some of us know better." Nick flexed his biceps. "Betsy Brunelle saw a fine male specimen and couldn't help herself. So you stick to your theories, Miss Marple."

"Did you just call me Miss Marple? She was, like, a hundred years old."

"Um, how about that Angela Lansbury character? What was her name?"

"Jessica Fletcher. Really? You think I look like Angela Lansbury?"

"No, I just can't think of any other female detectives. You're too old for Nancy Drew."

"You're just getting even with me for suggesting that Betsy might not have been hitting on you."

"No, not at all, sweetie. I'd never think of doing that. Hey, were there any women in those Charlie Chan movies?"

"No, why?"

"Because that way I could call you Number One Wife."

"Keep it up and you'll be looking for Number *Two* Wife."

"Hmmm … now you may be on to something."

Stella wadded the wax paper from her croissant and hurled it at Nick's head.

"Joking, joking," he laughed as he shielded his face with his hand. "So what's on tap for today?"

"I thought we'd start by checking in on our new neighbor, then follow it up with a shower at Alma's, a second visit with Alice, a chat with Jake Brunelle, and, finally, dinner."

"You think maybe we can fit a short hike in there somewhere?"

"A hike?"

"Yeah. I know you want to move this case along, but I didn't sign up for the all-murder-all-the-time channel."

"I know, but—"

"No buts. We're doing more than solving a mystery here, we're messing with people's lives. I want to find Weston's killer just as much as you do, but that doesn't mean I'm going to celebrate when we do."

Stella frowned. "You're right. I woke up in the middle of the night hoping that Alice or Alma or Mills isn't the killer. They've been so nice to us and … well, I've kinda grown to like them."

"Same here. Hell, given what we know about Weston, I'm pretty sure I'm going to feel bad no matter who gets arrested. Even crazy Hank Reid shouldn't be spending his final years in jail."

"And Josh Middleton is just a kid."

"I agree. That said, we're going to need a break. There's a brook that runs on this property just a few yards downhill from here. I say we walk down there later, before Alma comes for dinner, and clear our heads."

"Sure. When in Vermont …"

"You got it," Nick smiled. "Hey, speaking of dinner with Alma, I just thought of something."

"What?"

"If Alma's the murderer, she might not be cooking us dinner. She might be coming here to poison us."

"Well, it's a good thing she announced her dinner plans in front of the sheriff. That way, if we wind up dead, he'll know who did it."

"What if he's in on it? He could have put Alma up to killing us. He could have stolen the poison from the evidence room at the station. They could be running away together tonight. Could you imagine? Our bodies could be out here for weeks before anyone looks for us."

"Dinner had better be amazing, then," Stella deadpanned before wandering back inside the camp to change out of her pajamas.

STELLA AND NICK stood in the middle of Maggie Lawson's front sitting room and gazed in astonishment at the wild collection of objects that littered the area. To call it a sitting or living room was something of a misnomer, for newspapers, collectibles, paintings, photos, and books had been stuffed into every corner and stacked onto every available surface, thus leaving no space in which a human could sit and very little room for anything, save an insect, to live.

As Maggie shuffled around the adjacent dining room rearranging random items, Nick leaned in close to his wife and whispered, "Hey, is it just me, or does it feel like we should we be looking for the dude with the glasses and red-and-white-striped shirt?"

Stella shushed him. "I'm sorry I missed you the other day, Maggie. It was very kind of you to bring over those cupcakes."

"I know why you're here, ya know."

"Um, you do?"

"Yup. You want to know about my husband's treasure."

Nick leaned toward his wife and asked, sotto voce, "You want to board the crazy train first? Or should I do the honors?"

"I handled Reid; that makes this *your* party. Besides, if Betsy Brunelle is any indication, you have a way with women."

"You just had to go there, didn't you?" Nick cleared his throat and used his normal voice again. "So, what treasure are you talking about, Maggie?"

There was a pause from the other room. "The treasure my Mack found and hid under the stairs—the treasure Weston stole from me."

"Your husband found this treasure during his carting days?"

"Yup."

"And hid it under the basement stairs?"

"That's what I said, isn't it?"

"Sorry, just wanted to make sure I heard you correctly. It's not every day that someone finds treasure."

"'Course not. That's what makes it valuable."

"Well, that and denomination. How much money did Mack find, and where did he find it?"

"Money! Who said anything 'bout money? This was a genuine antique. Worth fortunes, too."

"What was it?"

"A painting. A painting of Saint John the Baptist."

"Who was the painting by?"

"Don't remember. Just know that Mack said it was worth a lot of money."

"I used to work at a museum," Stella spoke up. "If you describe the painting to me, I might be able to figure out who the artist was."

"Looked like John the Baptist."

"Aside from that ... what was John wearing? Was there anyone else with him? Was it daytime? Nighttime?"

"Can't rightly tell you."

"You don't remember what it looks like?"

"Never saw it." Something crashed to the floor as Maggie continued rearranging myriad objects.

Stella turned to her husband, her mouth the shape of a tiny *O*.

"Toot toot," Nick mimicked a train whistle. "All aboard."

"Um, I thought you said it was stored beneath the basement stairs."

"It was. Mack put it under the bottom step and then walled the whole thing up. Been using it as a closet for years."

"I know this might sound silly, Maggie," Nick asked carefully, "but if you never saw the painting, how do you know it's missing?"

Maggie came to the doorway and stared at Nick as if he were completely daft. "I crawled to the back of that closet, that's how. Shone a flashlight under the bottom steps, but there weren't nothing there."

"Maybe it got moved and was elsewhere in the closet?"

"Nope."

"Did you look?"

"Yep. Didn't see it."

"How can you be sure you didn't see it if you don't know what the painting looks like?"

"Know it's of John the Baptist. What else do I need to know?"

"I think I'm losing it," Nick said, scratching his head. "That actually made sense."

"I think what Nick was trying to say is if you've never seen the painting and you never saw Mack hide it, how can you be certain it was even under the steps in the first place? Or that it even existed?"

"Mack wouldn't have made up such a story. He spent his whole life picking through trash, and he finally got treasure. Remember it like it was yesterday. He came home grinning like a fox with his pick of the hen house. Said he'd found a treasure would take care of me long after he was gone. Told me he'd put it under the steps for safekeeping and that if he were to pass on before I did, I was to go down there and get it. When Mack died, I did exactly like he told me to, but it weren't there. If you don't believe me, go have a look for yourself."

Given the state of the front parlor, Stella was fearful of what they might find in the basement. "That's okay, we believe you. We don't need to go rummaging through your basement."

"No, we do not," Nick agreed. "However, now that you mentioned searching the basement, I can't help but wonder if maybe—just maybe—it isn't possible that Mack moved the painting and forgot to tell you?"

Maggie pursed her lips together and shook her head back and forth. "Mack wouldn't have forgotten to tell me something like that. Not something that important."

"I'm not saying he would, but—"

"No buts about it. That painting was here in this house 'til Allen Weston took it."

"You mentioned Weston earlier, but I still don't understand what you mean. If the painting was here, in this house, how did he get ahold of it?"

"When Mack died, he left this place a mess. Filled from floor to rafters with junk. Weston offered to help cart some of the stuff away for free."

"You mean this—what we're seeing right now—is clean? Wow."

Maggie merely glared at him.

"That was nice of Allen Weston to help you clean up this place," Stella remarked in an attempt to avert Maggie's ire. It didn't work.

"Nice? Least he could do for stealing my husband's business and putting him in an early grave!"

"What do you mean, stole the business? I thought Weston bought it. Legally."

"Oh, he bought it, all right. He bought it for not much more than a tired old dime. Mack was sick over it. He passed away four months later."

"I'm sorry, Maggie. I can't imagine what you've gone through, but I don't see where Weston is to blame. If anything, most people would consider Weston's purchase a smart business move."

"I don't. Weston was a cheat and a liar. He robbed me of my husband, and he robbed me of my treasure."

"You say Weston stole the painting when he carted away your"—Nick gestured to the piles of objects surrounding them—"stuff. How would he have known where the painting was or that it even existed?"

"Mack probably told him. He was a good man, my Mackie, but he never could keep his mouth shut. Especially if he was down at the grill with his hunting buddies."

"So you think Weston knew about the painting and offered his carting services as an excuse to get into your home and steal it?"

"Yep." Maggie folded her arms across her chest.

"Did you tell the police about your theory?"

"Sure did. Mills took the call, but he didn't do nothing. Didn't come out here to look around. Didn't talk to Weston. Nothing."

"In Mills's defense, it's tough to investigate the theft of something that no one has seen. I don't mean to be rude, but you reporting your painting as stolen is like telling the police that someone kidnapped Bigfoot. Even if they believed it existed, they still have no idea what it looks like."

"I may be a fool, but I'm not a damned fool. They knew what it looked like because I told them. I said *it's John the Baptist* time and time again. All they had to do was go to Weston's house or office or car and look for it. But did they? No."

"Have you tried talking to Mills about it personally? Outside of the sheriff's office?"

"No need. The Lord helps those who help themselves."

"So you've been looking for it on your own?"

"You betcha. Weston knew I was looking for it, too. Caught me a few times searching."

"On his property?"

"Yup, spotted me twice at the well shop and the junkyard, and then once at the septic service office."

"And he never called the cops?"

"Nope. Thought he would once or twice, but he didn't. Then I figured out why: because it ain't at any of those places."

"That's quite a stretch, don't you think?"

"Nope. Galls me that I had to run into him all those times, but seeing him made it all clear. Weston had the painting at his house."

"Why do you think that?"

"Makes sense, doesn't it? He wouldn't keep a thing like that where everyone and his brother could find it. Might get stolen again, right?"

"Assuming someone knew what it was worth."

"Oh, they'd know it was valuable the minute they saw it."

"But you never saw it. How would you …?" Nick scratched his head.

"If my Mack figured out it was worth something, it wouldn't take much for someone else to notice it too. Mack was a good man, but he weren't a genius. That's why I said it'd be an easy case for the police. All they'd have to do is get a warrant, get into Weston's house, and take the painting back."

"Did you tell the police your suspicions?"

"Hell, no. Unless I had a Polaroid picture of the thing, they weren't gonna do nothing. And you know why? I'll tell you why. Cause they didn't want to upset Mr. Weston and all his money. *Money.* Hmph! But now that Mr. Weston's gone, I can search all I like and he can't stop me."

"Yeah, I'm not sure if I'd go running over to his—"

Maggie seized a hunting rifle from the corner of the room and stroked it menacingly. "You trying to stop me from finding my treasure?"

"No! No, of course not," Nick said quickly. "Not if you feel that strongly about it."

"I think Nick was just saying that the police—"

"The police," Maggie sneered. "Are they on your side too? You paying them off to protect you the same way Weston did?"

"No," Stella said softly. "No, we're not. We're on your side."

"Yeah, so could you put down the gun, please?"

Maggie, however, was on a tear. "With all his money, you'd think he'd let an old woman have her treasure. But who got the last laugh? Where'd that money get him, huh? The bottom of your well, that's where."

As Stella and Nick snuck out the door of the Lawson house, they overheard Maggie's disturbing laugh. "How you like that painting now, Mr. Weston? How you like it now?"

Chapter
12

NICK BACKED OUT of Maggie Lawson's overgrown gravel driveway and drove, hell bent for leather, back into town.

"Still wondering why she's called Crazy Maggie?" Stella asked as she struggled to fasten her seat belt.

"No, I think I'm good."

"I'm glad, because we nearly got ourselves killed."

"I know. What's with this place, anyway? When I hear someone call an old widow crazy, I assume she's shuffling her feet, collecting cats, and talking to herself. Someone might have warned us that she's the NRA poster girl."

"I think Mills did warn us, didn't he? When he said not to get her riled up?"

"Yeah, but I thought he was exaggerating, didn't you? She brought us cupcakes, for chrissakes! And what does *riled up* mean, anyway?"

"We just saw what it meant."

"That wasn't riled up, that was trigger-happy."

"Well, apart from learning that Mills has a tendency to understate things, if anything came from that encounter, it's the realization that Maggie is a very viable suspect."

"That and we never want to go over there to borrow a cup of sugar."

"You can't borrow sugar from someone in jail. Think about it, Nick. Maggie fits the killer profile perfectly. She owns a hunting rifle, harbored a grudge against Weston, and only had to look out her window to see him pull into our driveway."

"It's only a half-mile walk from her house, too."

"Uh-huh. Close enough for her to march over there and shoot Weston, yet far enough for her to want to buy herself time to walk back—which would explain Weston's truck being parked in the woods."

Nick thought for a second. "You don't think Weston might have parked it there himself? I mean, Weston was working at our house alone and just a half mile away from a crazy woman who obviously had it in for him."

"Maggie told us that despite all her sneaking around, Weston never once called the cops on her. It's obvious that he didn't see her as a serious threat. If Weston himself parked the truck in the woods, it was because he didn't want to be bothered by her, not because he was afraid."

"Really? Because, personally, the woman scares the hell out of me."

"Me too, but it seems as though he was far too arrogant to be afraid of someone like Maggie Lawson. Anyone who steals a painting from someone's home in broad daylight while that person is at home has nerves of steel," Stella remarked.

"You don't honestly believe the painting is real, do you?"

"I don't know. Maggie seems to be convinced that it is, and she knew Mack better than anyone."

"Yeah, but Maggie also threatened to shoot us, remember?"

"Technically, she never really threatened. She just brandished."

"Good enough for me."

"So you don't think there's a painting?"

"Nope. I think Maggie and Mack were perfectly and crazily matched. Whatever one said, the other swore was true."

"Just like you and me," Stella teased.

"Oh yeah, I know I can always count on you to have my back. Just like this morning, when I said Betsy Brunelle hit on me."

"I believed you. I just thought you might have embellished the story a bit."

"Uh-huh. Anyway, my theory? Weston wasn't afraid of Maggie because he didn't steal the painting. Why? *Because it never existed in the first place.*"

"I suppose you could be right. That would also explain why the police never responded to Maggie's call. But either way, I can't help but laugh at the irony."

Nick's face registered confusion. "What irony?"

"That I left my job as a museum curator only to wind up looking for the head of John the Baptist in modern-day Vermont."

After a stop at Alma's doublewide to shower and change into clean clothes, Stella and Nick arrived at Vermont Valley Real Estate a few minutes before noon.

Alice Broadman, dressed in the weekend mom uniform of baggy jeans and oversized sweatshirt, was hunched over her desk, poring over pages of spreadsheets. A pair of red reading glasses, strikingly bright against her pale complexion, perched precariously on the tip of her nose.

"Alone, I see?" Stella noted as she stepped into the unlit office.

Alice looked up and, in an uncharacteristic indication of vanity, removed her glasses and stuffed them into a desk drawer. "Oh, hey. Yeah. Hard to believe, but during the housing boom I actually had to hire a weekend staff to answer the phones and handle walk-ins. Now? Bunny has weekends off and I"—she stood up to model her casual attire—"I've given up hope of anyone walking in off the street looking for anything but directions."

"Even during fall foliage?"

"Even during fall foliage. Gone are the days when tourists would come up here for a weekend, fall in love with the scenery, and immediately rush to find a vacation home. People are more cautious with their money now. They check the listings on the Internet, research the area, approximate taxes, look into caretaking fees … the only thing they need me for is to tour the property and finish the deal. But most of them break off their Vermont romance before they even reach that point."

"Is that what happened with the property in New Jersey?" Nick spoke up. "Did someone break off the romance?"

Alice's peaches-and-cream complexion turned an unhealthy shade of gray. "I—I don't know what you're talking about."

"Sure you do. Search your memory. Little place in Hackensack. Allen Weston put you up to the deal."

"How do you know all this?"

He eased into one of the two metal-framed chairs facing Alice's desk. "Doesn't matter how we know. What matters is that you lied yesterday."

"I didn't! I didn't tell you about the New Jersey property, but I didn't lie!"

"That sounds like an excuse your kids would use."

Stella sat beside her husband and, as they had discussed during the ride from Alma's, assumed the role of good cop. "Now, Nick," she said gently, "let's cut Alice some slack. She never actually denied doing business with Weston. What she said is that she never signed anything with Weston's name on it. Considering how the deal turned out, I believe that's probably quite true."

"Hmph. Care to tell us about it?"

Alice sat down slowly. "It's a condo building. Weston came to me last year, right around the time that the economy was at its worst. He wanted to buy the condo on short sale, fix it up, and then sell the units at a profit."

"What's a short sale?"

"It's the step prior to foreclosure. Buyers make their best offer to the seller, who, in turn, picks the highest offer and submits it to the mortgage-holding bank for approval. The bank decides whether or not they'll accept. If they do, the seller's debt is wiped clean and both he and the bank have avoided foreclosing costs and bankruptcy hearings."

"And the buyer gets a great deal without a lot of red tape."

"That's the idea, but it's not a sure thing. I certainly wouldn't suggest it to anyone who needs to close by a certain date, since the bank can always refuse your offer. The condo in Hackensack, however, was a business deal, so there was no rush. And the whole plan was incredible … or at least that's how Weston presented it."

"What happened?"

"Weston had a sizeable down payment to buy the building in Hackensack, but he couldn't get a loan because his most recent business acquisitions had overextended his credit. His partner in New Jersey, a man named Walker, ran a construction company that could fix the units at cost, but, like Weston, the economic downturn had made it impossible for him to secure a loan."

"So you have two partners with plenty of cash but zero credit."

"Exactly. So Weston came to me with an offer. He would make the down payment and pay me a $10,000 cash incentive if I would take the mortgage out in my name, with Walker as a cosigner. Once the sale was complete, I would then quitclaim the title to Walker so that he could get all the necessary permits and other items needed for the renovations without having to ask for my signature, and, in the end, we'd all split the profits from the sale of the units."

"In other words, he asked you to be a straw buyer," Stella interpreted.

Nick added, "I'm starting to think I need a real-estate license for this conversation. What's a straw buyer?"

"It's someone who uses their credit to get a mortgage for someone else," Stella replied. "I don't understand why would you agree to such a thing, Alice. Didn't you realize you were committing mortgage fraud?"

"Of course I realized that. But Weston had come to me right after the first layoff and, I'll admit it, his offer seemed like the miracle I had been praying for. The $10,000 was exactly what I needed to help the business stay afloat a little while longer, but the true temptation was the resale once the construction was finished. Naturally, I had my doubts about getting involved, but everything presented to me seemed to be on the up-and-up. Weston was fronting his own money for the down payment, and his friend in New Jersey sent me drawings, plans, and artists' renderings depicting what the units would look like after construction. The guy even sent me a copy of an invoice for an architect."

"So what went wrong?"

"Nothing—at first. The bank accepted our first offer even though it was unbelievably low. I got the loan, Weston's friend got the title, and work on the first few units was to be completed in three months so that we could start selling."

"Who was responsible for the mortgage payments during those first three months?"

"Weston put up the first month at closing. I paid the next two, but when the three months stretched into four, five, and six, I started to wonder what was going on. So I went to Weston to find out if he had heard from Walker. He said he hadn't but that he'd try to track him down."

Alice drew a deep breath. "Another month went by, and Weston still hadn't been able to reach Walker, so I decided to search for him myself."

"A private investigator?" Nick posited.

"No, I had a mortgage-broker friend of mine do a check on the title. The building had been resold ninety days after I had signed the quitclaim, at a price $300,000 more than what we had paid. The entire thing, the whole blasted plan, was a flopping scheme."

"Okay, again, in English."

"Flopping is like flipping, except you're ripping off the bank and your investors by buying below market value and then reselling for way more. And Weston was in on the flop from the beginning. He and Walker probably split the proceeds of the sale."

"Do you have proof Weston was in on it?"

"No, and I couldn't think of a way to get any either. But it's the only way the whole thing makes sense. Why else would he have been so willing to front his own money? And why was he so reluctant to track down Walker?" Alice blinked back the tears. "Weston had me as their mark from the beginning."

"Did you contact the police about your suspicions?"

"How can I?" Alice's tears broke free and streamed down her round, pink face. "Not only don't I have proof, but I'm guilty of mortgage fraud. Aside from losing my business and my broker's license, I could…I could go to jail. Weston knew it. He knew that even with the proper evidence, I couldn't blow the whistle."

"Did he tell you that when you asked him for money?"

Alice's tears dried and her pink face grew bright red with rage. "How did you—? That bitch Bunny told you, didn't she? She listened in during my meeting. I knew it! That nosy old bag! Why, I could—"

"It wasn't Bunny," Stella lied to diffuse the situation. "Weston wrote the meeting on his calendar."

Alice quieted down but was still highly skeptical. "And you just assumed I asked for money?"

"Given the circumstances you described, why else would you meet with him?"

"Okay, you're right: I *did* ask him for money. He refused. He said he didn't owe me anything and then started crying poverty because he had lost his down payment. When I told him I thought that he had been in on the scheme, he smiled. Can you believe it? The son of a bitch *smiled* and said that I was a businesswoman who should have known the risks."

"How did you react?" Nick asked.

"How do you think I reacted? I lost it. I started screaming, crying … I may even have hit Weston. I don't remember. All I know is that if Bunny weren't already listening at the door, she would have heard me, along with half the town."

"And Weston? What did he do when you starting yelling?"

"He was smooth, cool, as usual. He didn't lose his temper or shout back, he just laughed." Alice began to cry again. "The bastard laughed, asked me if my husband knew about our business arrangement, and then left."

"Did your husband know about the condo deal?"

"No, he would have talked me out of it, and I was … I was desperate to keep my agents working. I probably should have told him, but at the time I didn't think he needed to know. I hadn't used any of the household money, and I hadn't gambled our home. I figured if things went well, I could tell him when the money came rolling in. God, what a fool I was."

"And if Weston were to have told him about you committing mortgage fraud?"

"I don't know what he'd do. Him finding out was my worst fear. It still is. To have lost most of my business and my self-respect is one thing, but to lose him, the kids …" Alice ran a hand over her face. "When Weston left here that day, I was in a panic. I was so afraid he'd tell my husband what happened, I couldn't eat, couldn't sleep."

"Did you talk to Weston when he was working at our house?"

"Yes, I did. How did—?"

"Your timeline doesn't quite work out," Stella explained. "If you had left our house when you claim, you would have had plenty of time to make our closing. But instead you were late, out of breath, and more than a little bit frazzled."

"When I learned that Weston would be working on your well, I saw my chance to talk to him again. I begged him not to tell my husband, Tim, about the flop scheme, and then I asked him what it would take for him to keep his mouth shut."

"Is that why our appointment was rescheduled?" Nick asked. "So that you could meet up with him?"

"No, that was Weston's doing. If anything, I had more time to talk to him on Wednesday than on the day of your closing."

"But you still managed to find some time to talk to him, didn't you?"

"Yes. I had to."

"And how did it go?"

"How do you think? Weston didn't care that I could lose everything. He just didn't care. I was so mad, I could have—" Alice's testimony was interrupted by the loud ring of a telephone.

"Vermont Valley Real Estate," she answered in a perfect telephone voice. "Oh, yes … yes … no, I'm not busy. Just let me finish up with my secretary, will you? Thanks. Hold a moment, and I'll be right back."

Alice pushed a red button and covered the receiver. "This is an important call. I have to take it."

Nick looked at Stella and then rose from his chair. "We understand. I think we're pretty much done anyway."

"I suppose you're going to tell Mills everything I told you."

"I'm afraid we have to, Alice," Stella frowned.

"I didn't kill him. I swear I didn't."

"That's up to the sheriff's office to decide."

Alice nodded somberly. "I'll be here waiting for them. It's funny—as hard as I tried to keep Tim from finding out what happened, now that I'm here, on the verge of everyone finding out the truth, I'm relieved."

Nick smiled weakly. "I guess, deep down, part of you is tired of lying."

"I guess so. But that doesn't mean all is forgiven."

"What … ?"

"If you see Bunny this weekend, let her know she's fired." Alice, her eyes an icy blue color, let her finger hover over the red hold button. "Oh, and tell her to watch her back."

Chapter

13

STELLA GOT INTO the passenger seat of the Smart car and, despite the seventy-degree weather, began to shiver.

Nick slid into the driver's seat and put an arm around his wife. "You okay?"

"Yeah, it's just ... that woman's life is ruined. And it's all because we had to get involved."

"We might have helped to bring things out into the open, but the only one who ruined Alice's life is Alice."

"I know she's responsible for her own decisions, but she might have taken those secrets to her grave if we hadn't outed them. Now her husband might leave when he finds out, and she might go to jail, and her kids ... oh, her kids."

"She couldn't have kept it all a secret forever, hon. But this is exactly why I suggested we take a hike this afternoon. I had a feeling when we went to see Alice that the ending wouldn't be a happy one." He pulled his cell phone from inside his jacket and began pressing buttons.

"What are you doing?"

"Calling Mills to tell him to send his men over here."

"Oh, no, Nick! Don't call him now."

"Why not? Once he talks to Alice, we're free to go back to camp, go on our hike, and have a leisurely dinner with Alma. Isn't that what you wanted—to move into our house and put this mess behind us?"

"I did. I do, but…"

He pressed a few more buttons before flinging the phone into the center console in disgust. "You're in luck. I can't get a signal."

"See? Divine intervention. Let's just go see the Brunelles, and then we can call Mills afterward with all our findings."

"You want me to wait? And let Alice pack up her kids and skip town?"

"You heard her. She's not going anywhere."

"And you believed her? Hon, she lied to a mortgage company, her husband, her kids, and the whole community. Oh, and—hello—she's a murderer."

"I don't think she is."

"Why? Because she says she isn't? Newsflash: prison is full of people who claim they're innocent."

"I know that. I'm not naïve. But Alice being the murderer doesn't quite fit. It leaves too many unanswered questions."

"Like?"

"Like why was Weston's truck parked in the woods? Alice knew when our closing was going to take place, and she also knew that we weren't stopping by the house beforehand."

"So?"

"So, if Alice was the killer, she didn't need to delay discovery of the body while she made her getaway. No one was going to the house until the closing was finished, and, if someone did, they would no doubt call ahead, since Alice was the only one who held the key."

"Then Weston hid the truck himself."

"If so, it wasn't to hide from Alice Broadman. Weston's secretary called Alice personally to confirm his arrival at the house that morning. He could have parked his truck in Utah and Alice still would have known he was at the house. No, if Weston hid his truck, it's because there was someone out there—someone other than Alice Broadman—that he didn't want to see. And I suspect *that* person is the killer."

"I don't know, Stella. I think you're putting too much emphasis on the truck. Alice as the killer just seems right me. What about that threat she made toward Bunny?"

"Alice's life is falling apart, Nick. She's going to lash out, and since Bunny is the one who ratted her out, she's an obvious target."

Nick shook his head slowly. "I don't know ..."

"Okay, maybe I'm wrong about Alice, but I think we should at the very least talk to everyone in town and explore all the possibilities before we send the police breathing down her neck."

After a long pause, Nick pulled a face and started the car. "Which way to Jake Brunelle's shop?"

"Other side of town, by the trailer park."

He nodded and pulled onto Main Street. "So, just to check: Alice is still guilty of mortgage fraud, right?"

"Yes, Nick," Stella chuckled. "Yes, she is."

Jake Brunelle's shop occupied a former train maintenance depot on the edge of town near the park. Bearing no address, signs, or other markings to distinguish the building, Nick pushed open the shabby, weather-beaten front door, allowing Stella to poke her head inside.

Betsy Brunelle, wearing a tight black sweater dress, red lipstick, and several coats of mascara, sat at a desk fashioned from an old door and two sawhorses. At the creak of the front door, Betsy turned away from her computer screen and peered over her shoulder. "If you're looking for Brunelle Construction, you're in the right place."

"Thanks, we weren't sure," Stella explained.

"You're not the first. We've been meaning to put up the sign," she motioned to a cardboard box the size of a queen mattress that stood against the wall behind her. "Something else always comes up, though."

The couple stepped inside and closed the door behind them.

"Hey, you're that guy I bumped into this morning!"

Nick flashed his wife an I-told-you-so smirk before leaning forward to shake Betsy's hand. "Yes, I am. Nick Buckley, and this is my wife, Stella."

Betsy combed her shoulder-length chestnut-brown hair with her fingers before reaching a bangle-braceleted arm over her makeshift desk in greeting. "I'm Betsy Brunelle, Jake's wife."

"We know. Alma and Sheriff Mills told us your name when you stopped into the Sweet Shop yesterday morning."

"You were there yesterday? No, you couldn't have been. I would have noticed someone like you."

Stella cleared her throat and fought the urge to gag.

"I was there, sitting at the counter. You weren't in for very long, though—something about an estimate."

"That's right. If I hadn't wrestled Jake away from Sheriff Mills, we would have missed it, too. So you were at the counter, huh? I can't believe I didn't see you. I must have been in a terrible hurry not to notice a handsome new man in town."

Stella once again cleared her throat. "Sorry, something keeps tickling me."

"Would you like some water? I can—" She stopped what she was doing. "Wait one minute: water ... well ... .you own the place where they found Allen Weston's body, don't you?"

"Unfortunately, yes."

"Oh, that poor man. I swear this state needs stiffer gun laws. When anyone with a driver's license can get themselves a handgun, well, I can't believe we all aren't being murdered in our sleep."

"Weston was actually shot with a hunting rifle," Nick corrected.

"Really? Well, I don't think much of that either. Jake grew up here. He goes out every weekend during deer season, but I don't see what the attraction is." Betsy looked at Stella. "I grew up outside Boston, so when I want to unwind, I hit the mall for shopping therapy, if you know what I mean."

Stella laughed politely. "Tough to do that around here, though."

"Oh, I drive to Rutland, or if I'm really ambitious, over the border to New Hampshire. I refuse to resort to wearing flannel and rubber shoes."

"I think I'd have a tough time with that, too."

"So," Betsy sat back down. "Don't tell me: you're here because you need someone to finish that well work Weston started."

"Yep, you, um, you guessed it."

Betsy opened up the calendar on her computer and started look-ing at dates. "I might be able to squeeze you in next week."

From where Stella stood, prior to the coming Monday, the Brunelles' calendar had been relatively empty. The remainder of the calendar, however, had filled in nicely. A result of Weston's pre-mature demise?

"I'm not sure that would work," Nick responded. "The whole property is cordoned off—even to us—and I'm not sure when we'll be able to get back in."

Betsy took her hand off the mouse and placed it on Nick's. "Really? You mean you came all the way up and haven't been able to move in or to carry your lovely bride over the threshold?"

"Nope. Didn't even get to unload the moving van."

"That's terrible. And all because of a silly hunting accident?"

"The police aren't totally convinced it was an accident."

Betsy suddenly removed her hand from Nick's. "But you said Weston was shot with a hunting rifle."

"He was."

"What? They think it might be suicide?"

"No, more like murder."

"That's impossible. This is a small town. No one even bothers to lock their doors at night. Who would even think to do such a thing?"

"Don't know, but from what we've heard, Weston had plenty of enemies in this town. Even—no, I shouldn't say it ..." Nick scratched his head and looked down at his feet.

Betsy's brown eyes grew wide with curiosity. "Say what?"

"No, I can't."

"Go ahead and say it."

"Well, you and Jake were mentioned as possible suspects. Seems people think you both had an axe to grind with Weston for taking business away from you."

"That's ridiculous. Sure, he was our competitor, but our business is still doing very well. This is Vermont. Around here, most contractors don't even return your phone call. If you show up for the estimate and start on time, you're halfway to success."

Stella watched as Betsy's ancient computer monitor launched into a screensaver of handsome cowboys engaging in a variety of rodeo activities. "According to Hank Reid, Weston was pretty good at keeping his appointments. What's more, Weston advertised that he had the manpower to get the job done quickly. If a man like Hank Reid fell for Weston's fancy ads and promises of fast service, I'm sure others must have, too."

"Maybe, but they'll all wind up like Hank Reid: in court with Weston but back doing business with us. The fact is, Weston was a liar and a cheat. People may have fallen for his lines at first, but they eventually wised up."

"It doesn't matter any longer whether they wise up or not now, does it?"

"Well, I—I guess not. But if Weston were still alive, the customers who switched to him would figure out the truth behind his promises and realize what they had with us."

"So you admit that you lost other customers," Nick said with a smile.

Betsy leveled a stare that could have burned a hole through his chest. "Okay, yeah, we lost some customers to Weston. But the ones who switched weren't our best customers anyway. They were the ones who always tried to nickel-and-dime us and drive our prices down. The good ones—the ones who know that good work takes time—remained loyal."

"Still, even losing your 'lesser' customers must have hurt your bottom line. Why else would you have closed up all winter?"

"How did you—? Wait, Hank probably told you that, too."

"Does it matter? We could have found out from anyone."

"Fine. Yes, we did close for business this past winter, but spring and summer put us back on track. In fact, we were so busy that I hired Elizabeth Randall to help me in the office on weekends."

"You had that much business?"

"A couple of bigger jobs, yes. She managed the phones and did some filing, which gave me some time away from this place." Betsy eyed the walls with disgust and then leaned across her desk. "Do you two work together?"

Nick and Stella shook their heads.

"Then you wouldn't understand, but Jake and I live in the apartment upstairs. Living and working in the same place and with the same person? It gets old—fast. I don't care how great your marriage is, it takes its toll."

"I can't imagine how difficult that would be," Stella sympathized. "If I saw Nick every moment of every day, I'd go crazy!"

Nick gave her a hurt look before jumping back into the questioning. "Why isn't Ms. Randall here now? It's a Saturday."

"I had to let her go."

"Because business slowed down?"

"Um, well, our big jobs drew to a close, yes. But it wasn't all about the money, you know. She had some … rotten habits. Want another piece of advice? Don't work with friends, either. The things your girlfriend does that normally make you laugh can cause you headaches in the office."

"Duly noted," Stella remarked.

"So, not to be insensitive, but now that your big jobs have finished up, Weston's death is sure to come in handy."

"What do you mean?"

"Well, you've probably already gotten some calls from Weston's customers."

"We've gotten a few bookings, yes," Betsy acknowledged.

"A few? Come on. You're the only other contractor in town. Even though Weston's guys could probably handle the work on their own, without a signature to put on their paychecks, I doubt any of them are going to break a sweat. Likewise, I don't think the homeowners who booked Weston would want to go ahead with their plans either. God forbid something goes wrong—like a floating septic tank, for example. Who are they going to sue? A dead man?"

"Hold on tight to this one, Stella. He's as smart as he is cute," Betsy said with a wink in Nick's direction.

Not all the time, thought Stella as she watched Nick being sucked into Betsy Brunelle's web of flattery.

"All right, if you must know, we have gotten some calls from Weston's customers. And we're running an ad in tomorrow's paper ... you know, offering to honor his contracts. It might not feel like it today, but we're coming into winter. People want their projects done before the holidays and prior to the ground freezing. They're not going to wait around and see what happens with Weston's businesses."

"That's a great marketing angle. Whose idea was it?"

"Mine, of course. Jake never—" She was interrupted by the sound of a car door in the parking lot. "Oh, here he is now."

Stella and Nick stepped away from the door to allow Jake Brunelle admittance.

"Hey" was his single-word greeting.

"Hey, baby," Betsy welcomed. "These are the Buckleys."

"Hi. We actually saw you at Alma's the other morning. I'm Nick," said Nick, offering his hand.

Jake stared at it with an expression somewhere between amusement and contempt and continued to walk into the back shop area. "Weston get to fixing your well before he bit it?"

"No, of course he didn't," Betsy said nervously. "That's why Nick and his wife, Stella, are here."

"Hmph. Did you set up an appointment?"

"We were just doing that when you walked in."

"Yes," Stella confirmed. "I'm not sure when to schedule you to do the work, though, since we're locked out until the police find Weston's murderer."

Jake Brunelle stopped cold in his tracks. "Murder, huh? Willing to lay money on it being a hunting accident."

"You and the rest of the town," Nick quipped.

"Guess that's what happens when you own a big house up on Windsor Hill. People kill you to try and get your money."

"Or even your business."

"I don't think I like what you're suggesting there, Nick."

"Who's suggesting? I'll say it outright: Weston's death is good for your business. End of story."

"I come in here to find you eyeing up my wife, and you have the nerve to insult me?"

"Eyeing up your wife? Don't be ridiculous!"

"Well, you were kinda flirting, Nick," Stella pointed out.

"Not helping, honey. Look, even if I had been flirting with your wife, *my* wife is standing right next to me."

"Didn't say you were smart."

As Nick stewed, Betsy moved to her husband's side and rubbed his back soothingly. "Jake, baby, you know when you lose your temper, no good comes of it. Mr. Buckley wasn't doing anything wrong. He was being very polite and friendly."

"Yeah, it was *your* wife who—" Stella was about reveal that it was Betsy who had been doing the ogling but thought better of it. "You know what? I think we'll just be going."

"I'd listen to your wife there, Nick. She's right, you'd best be going. And if I catch you drooling over my wife again, you'll be sorry," Jake threatened before marching to the back of the shop.

Nick opened his mouth to reply, but Stella shook her head in warning. "Don't, Nick. Let's just go."

He backed down and followed his wife to the door, where Betsy gave them each a business card in parting. "I know he can be rude, but he does really good work. If you can't find someone to fix your well, just give us a call. I'll take 15 percent off the price, and I won't tell him it's you."

Stella could not believe her ears. "Ummm … thanks." She made the statement sound more like a question.

Nick, however, refrained from comment until, having tossed his keys to his wife, he was safely settled in the passenger seat of the Smart car, whereupon he held his business card aloft. "Look, honey: 15 percent off. Just think, when Stable Mable in there finishes with our well, we can use the money we saved to hire Mel Gibson to paint our living room. We'll call it *Crazy Contractor Week at the Buckleys'*."

"Sounds like an HGTV special."

The summerlike temperatures, combined with the strong sunshine, had rendered the automobile uncomfortably warm. Stella rolled down the driver's-side window with a sigh. "Whew!"

Nick followed suit. "Hey, I'll take the heat over talking to crazies any day. I don't know which was more uncomfortable—Maggie waving a gun at us or Jake Brunelle accusing me of making a move on his wife."

"Personally, watching Betsy give you a full-body massage with her eyeballs was even more disconcerting than being held at gunpoint." Stella pulled out of the Brunelles' parking lot and made a right-hand turn.

"I told you she hit on me this morning."

"You did, and you were right. I'm sorry. Hitting on you while you were at Alma's is one thing, but you think she might have scaled it back a bit just now—you know, considering I was actually in the same room this time."

"Yeah, that was ... "

"Crazy?"

"Crazy as in Maggie Lawson's trigger-happy crazy?"

"No, more like *Fatal Attraction* crazy."

"Hey, just because a woman thinks I'm hot doesn't make her crazy. Look at you."

"Honey, your mother and brother told me about your ex-girlfriends; I'd say I'm the exception to the rule. But Betsy Brunelle? She tops even your ex-girlfriends. She's a different kind of crazy altogether. I can't figure it out … it was almost as if she was trying to get a reaction."

"Well, she got one. Jake Brunelle was ready to beat the living daylights out of me."

"Eh, you could have taken him."

"That's right. Unless, of course, he brought his dwarf axe with him."

"In Jake's defense, he probably acts that way because he knows what his wife is like. It's easier for him to lash out at other men than to lose his wife's affection."

"I don't know. If you did that to me, I'd have no problem letting you know I was unhappy."

"Yes, but they have a different dynamic than we do. It's apparent that Gimli—er, Jake—relies on Betsy to run his business."

"Really? It seemed to me as if she was scared of him, what with the way she greeted him."

Stella shook her head. "She's scared of his outbursts and what he might do when he loses his temper, but she's not scared of him. She has too much control."

"Control? Really? I didn't get that."

"Sure. Betsy takes care of the office, devises the marketing campaigns, runs the ads, acts as spokesperson, and even makes sure Jake gets to his estimates on time. Jake does the work, but she drives the business. We were on our way out the door and she was still trying to get us to sign them to do our well work."

"And what does Betsy get out of the deal?"

"Same thing my mother did: money, shopping sprees, financial security…"

"And the flirting? What's up with that?"

"She's probably bored. Not only is her husband rough around the edges, but she gets to see that roughness every day, nearly all day."

"Hmmm. You think you'll ever get bored of me?"

"So long as every woman you meet is undressing you with their eyes, I don't see how I possibly could."

Nick grinned. "Betsy was driving you nuts back there, wasn't she?"

"Only every single time she looked, touched, or spoke to you," Stella replied with mock cheerfulness.

"Yeah, I thought so; you don't exactly have a poker face. The question is, did Betsy drive Jake nuts too? If what you're saying is true—that she's the driving force behind the business—she might have been pushing Jake to do something about Weston."

"We saw for ourselves that it doesn't take much to move him to violence. I wonder how far he'd go if Betsy left him unchecked."

"Or if Betsy had put the bug in his ear to begin with."

Stella made a sudden turn onto Main Street.

"Um, honey?" Nick said. "You're going the wrong way. You should have made a left."

"I know where I'm going."

"Not if we're heading to Perkins, you don't."

"Who said we were heading to Perkins?" Stella asked.

"We did. This morning. To see if they have an AC adapter for the mattress, remember?"

"Of course I do, but there's something we need to do first."

Nick groaned. "Oh, no. The last time you said that, we wound up in Guadalajara."

"Where else was I going to find an authentic mariachi costume? Certainly not in Acapulco."

"Our cruise ship left without us."

"But we had a good time waiting for the next one."

"I guess … so, what do we need to do this time?"

Stella paused for effect. "Check out Weston's house."

"No, we don't."

"Yes, we do."

"Why?"

"A few reasons. First, I want to see for myself if Maggie's painting is there."

"Not that again. Didn't we both agree that it was useless to search for something that may or may not exist?"

"We did, but Maggie was so convinced—not only that the painting existed, but that Weston stole it. I think she deserves to have someone at least look into it."

"It's not our fault no one looked into it. When you're named Crazy Maggie, people just don't put much stock in her claims."

"She didn't give herself that name," Stella mentioned.

"Yes, she did. She got it the minute she started waving guns around."

"Maybe she just waves guns around because she's frustrated. She obviously misses her husband, and the police don't believe her treasure story—I'd be frustrated, too."

"There are better, safer ways to deal with frustration—like yoga, for instance. But, moving on, what are your other reasons for wanting to see Weston's place?"

"I'd like to get some better insight into the man himself."

"You mean aside from the fact that he was a grade-A jerk?"

"Yes. It's a rather one-dimensional view, don't you think?"

"Not if it fits."

"You're right, maybe that's all Weston was: a jerk. But on the off chance he had a family, donated to charities, or had some other secret component to his life, I'd like to find out what it was."

"Uh-huh, because a guy who commits mortgage fraud might be a benefactor to a school for orphaned boys."

"No, but there had to be something he cared about—something that drove him to do the things he did."

"Stella, I know you like to think the best of people, but Weston seems like the sort of guy who didn't need a reason, apart from money, to do the things he did. He hurt people in order to get ahead and line his own pockets."

"You're probably right."

"Well, not necessarily; I just know the type. But if you feel you need to dig deeper and find out what made this guy tick, you know I'll go with you."

"Even if it means breaking and entering?"

"You had to go there, didn't you?" Nick sighed. "Yes, even if it means breaking and entering. My god, I can't believe I just said that. That's exactly what I said when you talked me into going to Guadalajara. What the hell is wrong with me?"

"You're standing by your wife. I don't see anything wrong with that."

"Of course you don't."

Stella merely shrugged.

"Have you happened to give any thought as to how you're going to find Weston's house?"

"Josh Middleton said that Weston lived on Windsor Hill. There's only seven or eight roads in this whole town. I figure if we pick the one that leads to Windsor Hill, we'll—aha!"

Nick looked up to see a street sign that read Windsor Hill Road. "Unbelievable. If I had tried that, we'd be driving for hours."

"That's because you don't have *the skills*," she teased as she navigated the Smart car onto the narrow dirt road and followed it uphill.

After approximately a mile of twists and turns, they encountered a driveway marked with a white rock upon which WESTON had been stenciled in bold, black letters. Given the descriptions of the Weston residence, one would have thought he had built himself a 4,000-square-foot mansion. At the end of the driveway, however, stood a brand-new, vinyl-shingled, two-story home built in the Colonial style. Surrounding it stood acre upon acre of pristine forest.

Although not large from a New York City perspective, it was quite lavish by Vermont standards. In addition to neoclassical columns that flanked either side of the front door and rose to support the roof of a wide portico, and beyond the verdant front lawn outlined with shrubs and trees of varying heights, colors, and textures, the most impractical feature of the Weston residence, by local standards, was that its cathedral ceilings would have required a good deal of oil or firewood in order to retain heat during the long New England winters.

Stella parked the car outside the two-door garage and, with Nick at her side, walked along the marble-lined path to the front door. Like their farmhouse well, it had been cordoned off with yellow police tape.

"What now, Columbo?" Nick posed.

"There must be a window we can jimmy open."

"Okay, hold on. You're talking about breaking and entering again."

"Yes, why? Do you have a better idea?"

"Uh, yeah. How about we stand outside and look through the windows?"

Stella sighed in exasperation. "We'll never find anything useful that way. I'll just see if I can find a way in. If not, we'll leave, and I'll forget about the whole idea."

"Okay. But did you happen to think that the police might have taken everything pertinent to the case out of the house?"

"Yes." She stopped along the breezeway that ran between the house and, suddenly bending down, emptied a two-foot square blue recycling bin of its contents and placed it, upside down, beneath a small first-story window on the side of the house. "But what they think is pertinent and what I think is pertinent might be two different things."

"Of *course*." He rolled his eyes.

Stella stepped onto the recycling bin and pushed in on the metal frame of the window screen. The entire unit popped out and fell onto the blacktop driveway, spurring her to swivel her hips in a victory dance and laugh maniacally. "Maybe I missed my calling! Maybe I should have been a cat burglar!"

"Yep, you're a regular Grace Kelly."

"Grace Kelly wasn't the thief, Cary Grant was," Stella corrected as she opened the bottom sash of the window. "Okay, keep watch. I'm going in."

"I can't believe we're doing this. You have seriously lost your mind."

Stella stuck her head through the open window and found herself peering into a futuristically styled powder room. Gleaming with stainless-steel fixtures and industrial gray tile, the only concession to traditional design was an enormous vanity mirror encased in an intricately carved silver-leaf frame.

After shimmying her hips through the narrow space, Stella sat on the window ledge, swung her legs inside, and jumped to the ground with a proud grin.

Let's see Miss Marple or Jessica Fletcher do that, she thought to herself before heading out of the powder room and into the pristine whiteness of the main foyer. There, much to her surprise, she discovered Nick, arms folded across his chest, waiting for her.

"What the—? How did you get in?"

Nick hiked a thumb toward the heavy, six-paneled front door. "It was unlocked. Apparently not even the cops bolt their doors around here."

"Are you serious? It was open the whole time?"

"Yep. Gotta love crime in rural areas, don't you? Some hunter could mistake us for turkeys, shoot us in the chest, and leave us to die, but, hey, at least our DVD player is safe."

"Fabulous. I know I'm relieved. I'm also ecstatic to learn that I crawled through a bathroom window for nothing."

"Eh, I don't know. You were kinda like Catherine Zeta-Jones in that thief movie—only blond, of course."

"Finally, a reference I can get behind."

"So can I—the view was quite nice. So, where are we headed?"

"Upstairs. Weston's bedroom. I figure if Weston was hiding anything, that's where we'd find it."

"No argument there, but may I remind you that Weston was a bachelor. It could be scary."

"I'll take my chances," she asserted before leading the way up the bare wooden staircase. At the top, she turned right, into a medium-sized bedroom with beige walls and clean white furnishings that felt altogether too feminine and small in scale to be the lair of such a dominant personality as Allen Weston.

Turning on one heel, Stella went back into the hallway and examined the bedroom to the left of the stairs. With its imposing size, dark walls, black padded leather headboard, and graphite-colored comforter, this space could most certainly be dubbed a man cave. But possibly the biggest clue to the gender of the room's primary inhabitant was the number and quantity of technological gadgets that occupied every visible surface: satellite clock radio with an iPod docking station, a white-noise generator, flat-screen television with surround sound, and a Bose audio system.

"Sweet," Nick exclaimed.

"I'll have our bedroom hooked up like this just as soon as we can move into it."

"Really?"

"Sure. Just as soon as I can hire a full-time manicurist, masseuse, and refrigerator cleaner."

"Refrigerator cleaner?"

"Why not? I don't mind vacuuming, dusting, and all the other stuff, but I truly hate cleaning the refrigerator."

"Aim high, honey."

Stella ignored him and went directly to the master bathroom's medicine cabinet. "Hmmm…" she said aloud while taking mental inventory.

"What? Something interesting in there?"

"Oh, the usual: Tylenol, toothpaste, toothbrush, dental floss…"

"There you go. You were looking for something positive to say about Weston, and now you have it. The guy might have been a jerk, but he was a jerk with great dental hygiene."

"Retinol cream, minoxidil, personal trimmer…"

"He was also getting wrinkles and fighting male pattern baldness while, ironically, combating nose and ear hair." Nick's eyebrows furrowed. "Damn, how old *was* this guy?"

"Tums, Rolaids, Mylanta, lorazepam…"

"Stress. And for obvious reasons: he was losing his hair, youth, hair, good looks, hair…"

"Male enhancement cream, Viagra…"

"No, seriously, hon. How old was this guy?"

"Forty-eight," she replied without missing a beat. "Condoms…"

"Ah, okay, so he was hitting something younger. Good… good."

Stella glared from around the corner of the bathroom door.

"No, no, I don't mean it that way. It was just getting kind of depressing there for a while, that's all."

"And, finally, Axe deodorant and Axe body spray."

"Axe? Maybe I should get some of that."

Stella lifted the cap of the deodorant and inhaled. "No. No, you shouldn't."

Nick took the can from Stella's hand and sniffed it. "Whew. You're right, I shouldn't."

Meanwhile, Stella had moved to Weston's closet. "Look at this. Do you see anything strange?"

"Yeah, it's all suits, dress shirts, and khakis."

"Meaning…?"

"Uh, Weston was a metrosexual?"

"That was a gimme considering the medicine cabinet. Apart from that?"

"He had a bigger wardrobe budget than you do?"

"Again, yes, but not the answer I was looking for. My first observation was that everything here is either a suit, dress shirt, or khaki. My second observation? Everything here has a designer label."

"So?"

"So, why was Weston's body found wearing a no-name flannel shirt and jeans?"

Chapter

14

THEIR SEARCH FOR the painting having turned up empty, Stella and Nick replaced the bathroom window screen at Weston's home and drove directly to Perkins in search of an AC car adapter.

The elderly clerk was once again on duty. "A what?"

"An adapter that fits into a car cigarette lighter," Nick explained.

"Nope. Can't say I have one of those."

"Can you think of anyplace else I could check?"

"There's a small electrical shop twenty miles from here."

"Great."

"But they're closed on the weekends."

Nick ran a hand through his short-cropped dark hair and sighed. "Okay, here's the deal. My wife and I bought the old Colton place—"

"Yup, I know."

"But, since we can't stay there—"

"Yup."

"We bought an air mattress and pump here, in your store—"

"Yup."

"Only to discover that—"

"Ray Johnson's place don't have electricity!" The clerk completed the sentence with a boisterous laugh.

"You knew that all along and yet you didn't say anything?"

"If I had, you wouldn't have bought the mattress."

"How neighborly of you."

"I'm not in business to solve problems. I'm in business to sell things. But I'll tell ya what. Since there's nothing wrong with the mattress or the pump, I can't refund your purchase, but I can let you plug in the pump and blow up the thing here."

"You want me to inflate an air mattress in your shop?"

"Yup."

"And then take it back to the camp … somehow."

"Yup."

"You're not going to charge me, are you? You know, since you're in business to sell things."

"Nope, it's on the house. If you spring a leak and need to re-inflate though, that's a different story."

"Naturally." Nick looked at his wife. "What do you think?"

"Oh, just do it," Stella replied.

TWENTY MINUTES LATER, the Smart car crept out of the Perkins parking lot, hazard lights flashing, the inflated air mattress balanced on the roof. Stella, her right arm through the passenger-side window, held the front right corner, and Nick, his arm through the driver's-side window, held the left.

"Why couldn't we have gotten the moving truck?" Stella asked as they turned slowly onto Route 4.

"We can't fit another thing in that truck. Besides, I didn't want Grandpa Walton in there to change his mind about using the pump."

"A gas station air compressor would have worked, wouldn't it?"

"Yeah, but the gas station is on the other side of town. Do you feel like driving another five miles with this thing on the roof?"

"Considering we're traveling at fifteen miles an hour, no thanks. I'd like to get back to camp before nightfall."

Their trip having taken three times longer than usual, Nick and Stella arrived back at camp and pulled beside a familiar pickup truck.

Alma, her dark hair twisted into its usual plait, sat on the front porch between a large plastic cooler and a hibachi. She had traded the previous day's *Country Living* look and the morning's "Mel's Diner" garb in favor of a Gap-inspired ensemble of beige chinos, a white T-shirt, and a lightweight denim jacket. As Nick and Stella stepped out onto the makeshift parking area, she rose from her Adirondack chair to greet them.

"You two won't soon die from boredom. Why didn't you tell me you needed to inflate that thing? We could have brought it back in my truck."

Stella and Nick stared at each other, their mouths in the shape of large *O*s.

"Well, at least it isn't raining," Alma laughed. "Come on. I'll help you get that in the house, and then we can start our barbecue."

Grabbing hold of the corners and side, the trio carried the unwieldy mattress indoors and returned to the front porch where, as the rays of the setting sun seemed to set the forest ablaze, Alma set about retrieving cold beers from the cooler. "Got some steaks and potatoes to grill up, and I threw together a salad from what's left in my garden. Nothing fancy, but I'm sure you've heard about our New England frugality."

"I have, but it doesn't seem accurate. You and everyone else have been very generous," Stella said.

"Well, I admit to pinching my pennies 'til they bleed at times, but that's just plain practicality. It doesn't make us mean or stingy, but add it to the list of misconceptions. When you mention Vermont, everyone thinks of those rubes on that Bob Newhart show. I admit, there are some folks up here who look like that, but they're not dumb—not dumb by a long shot. And if another person asks me if I've met Ben or Jerry, I might just scream. Ben and Jerry's ice cream might have originated in Vermont, but it's not the ice cream Vermonters eat."

"What is?"

"Everyone has their favorites, depending on which part of the state you live in, but for my money, Wilcox is the best. They sell it in store freezer cases now, but if you head south to the Wilcox Dairy Farm, you can have your cone in the middle of the cow fields. Doesn't get much better than that."

"Makes me want to grab one right now."

"Better hurry: they close after this weekend; most outdoor things do. Might seem like summer now, but once this passes it'll get cold fast. Then town will be overrun with skiers and snowboarders."

Nick withdrew his pocketknife and set about opening the bottle caps. "How long does this weather usually last?"

"If we're lucky, a couple of days, but typically five minutes," Alma joked and raised her beer bottle. "Welcome to Vermont."

The three of them swigged back the ice-cold beer before settling into the trio of Adirondack chairs.

"So, what did you folks do today?" Alma asked, the tone of her voice making it seem like more than just a casual question.

"Oh, this, that, and the other," Stella replied vaguely.

"Why do I get the feeling you've been out stirring up trouble?"

"Guess that depends on who you ask," Nick answered.

"No, I'm pretty sure that's everyone you ask. Whole town's talking about you being some kind of undercover detectives."

Stella laughed and wondered who might have started such a rumor. Middleton, perhaps? "No, we're, um, we're definitely not detectives."

"Then why are you so interested in this whole Weston business?"

"We just want it all cleared up so we can move into house and get on with our lives. And, as much as we admire and respect your police force—"

"I know. They're not as fast as in the city; nothing here is. But they do a good, thorough job."

"We don't doubt it," Nick stated. "But when you're waiting to empty your moving truck, it's tough to sit back idly and watch."

"So you swear you're not working for the police at all?"

"I swear."

"So anything I tell you won't go back to Sheriff Mills?"

"We can't promise that. If you're passing along a piece of information, fine. But if you're confessing to a crime . . ."

"Hell no, the only crime I've ever been guilty of is lack of judgment."

"Then go ahead. Your secret's safe with us."

Alma took a swig of beer and then sighed. "I guess there's no other way to say it than to just come out with it: I was seeing Allen Weston."

"Romantically?"

Alma nodded.

"How come you haven't mentioned it before?" Stella asked.

"He and I had agreed to keep it quiet. I had been through a rotten time in my marriage, and Allen was seven years younger than I am. I didn't want people to know about our relationship in case it didn't work out."

"Judging from your description of Weston yesterday morning, I'd say it didn't."

"Nope. I tell ya, of all the times in my life to pick to be right—Allen Weston turned out to be a weasel, just like everyone said. I was just too stupid to see it."

"What happened?"

"We were okay for the first little while. Like I said at the bakery, Allen could be a charming man. Wasn't bad-looking either; most men his age are losing their hair or have a beer gut. Not Allen. He looked great for his age."

Nick opened his mouth to comment on the minoxidil they had found in Weston's medicine cabinet.

Stella shot him a warning glance. "Not to interrupt you, Alma, but would you say that Weston—er, Allen—was a sharp dresser?"

"Oh, absolutely. Everything he wore was just so. Even his casual pants had a sharp crease to them."

"So he wasn't a flannel-and-jeans sort of guy?"

"I don't think he even owned a pair of jeans. And flannel, to him, was for rednecks."

"Thanks. Go ahead with your story. You and Allen began seeing each other..."

"Yes, and everything was good until about a month or so into the relationship. That's when he started talking about how successful my Sweet Shop was and asking if there was a way he could buy a partnership in it. I told him no. I didn't need a business partner, and if I did, it sure wouldn't be someone I was dating.

"Well, Allen wouldn't take no for an answer. Every time we got together he'd propose another deal. At first it didn't bother me. He was a businessman; he enjoyed wheeling and dealing. But after a while, I started to think that the only reason he started seeing me was so that he could get hold of my business."

"Did you confront him about it?"

"Oh yeah, he'd deny it and go out and do something to make me feel foolish for even mentioning it, like send me roses or surprise me with dinner. Then I'd drop the subject. It wasn't like I had any proof that he was trying to scam me. He was always doting on me when we were together, and the sex was great"—again Nick opened his mouth, only to have Stella glare at him—"but it seemed fake. It *felt* fake. It felt like it was all a big front. Like he was acting that way to get close to me and then act out his true intentions. Things went on like that for a few months until, a week ago, my neighbor, Bunny, came over for coffee. She got to gossiping, as she usually does, and mentioned that she saw Weston outside of town with a woman in his car."

Nick spoke up. "So? It could have been a client."

"Normally I'd agree with you, but Allen was supposed to be out of town on vacation at the time. When he 'got back,' I asked him how his vacation had gone. He said it was fine and that he had missed me, but he mentioned nothing about being in town."

"Bunny could have been mistaken," Stella suggested. "Lots of men around here have beards."

"No. Bunny's a snoop, but she's a reliable snoop. Eyes like an eagle and ears like a bat. If she said she saw Allen, then she saw Allen."

"Might she have said what she did to be vindictive?"

"She had no idea I was seeing Weston. I always arranged to meet him at his house, and it was never on the same day or at the same time."

"You're positive she had no clue of your relationship? Because she told us that she had seen you and Weston flirting with each other."

"You spoke to her, then? Ha, she wastes no time, does she? I'm positive she had no clue about the relationship. Flirting, sure, but as far as she was aware, that was the extent of it. If she thought otherwise, she would have said something. She can't keep a lid on that mouth of hers to save her soul."

"Did she tell you who the woman in the car was?" Stella asked.

"She didn't get a good look at her. Allen was driving in the opposite direction as Bunny. When they passed each other on the road, Allen looked right at her, but the woman hunched down in her seat."

"Did you confront Allen about it?"

"No, I figured it was time to move on."

"So you broke up with Weston over a woman whose identity you don't know," Nick summarized.

"No, there was the business thing too. But if you're asking if the woman was the straw that broke the camel's back, absolutely. I realize it sounds strange, but I've known Bunny a lot longer than I'd known Allen. And, to be honest, I hadn't trusted him in months. I guess I was looking for something to put the nail in the coffin. Bunny's story did the trick."

"When did you break up with him?"

"Earlier this week. I went to his office pretending to want an estimate on a new well."

"How did Allen take it?"

Alma's eyes welled with tears. "He shrugged and said 'That's too bad.' Then he said he had to get back to work. That's it ... nothing else—no *stop, I love you*. Just a shrug and a *get lost*."

"You poor thing," Stella said sympathetically. "To think you wasted your time on such a jerk."

"Yeah, that's too bad," Nick spoke up. "But why are you telling us all this?"

"I'm not a stupid woman. Allen's reaction gives me a reason for wanting him dead. But I also know it's better that I tell you everything now than to have you find out on your own."

"Yeah, I get that. What I mean is, why us? Why not go to the police? Why not tell Sheriff Mills?"

Alma looked up in fear. "He already knows."

"He does?"

"Well, I'm not sure he knows the details, but it was the morning after I broke up with Allen. I had been up all night crying, so you could imagine what a mess I was. Mills showed up at his usual time, but it was raining, so I let him in before opening. I tried to be strong, I really did, but I eventually broke down and told him what had happened. Before I could even finish the story, he was off his stool and out of the shop."

"What day was this?"

"The day before you arrived. The day before Allen was killed."

Stella felt her heart nearly leap out of her chest. Was it possible that the sheriff had killed Weston—not out of jealousy but out of vengeance for the woman he loved?

"Did you see Mills the next morning?" Nick continued.

"Yes, he showed up at his usual time. Like always."

"How was he?"

"Things were a bit awkward at first. I apologized for my outburst, and he excused me, like I knew he would. He said he understood what I was going through, assured me that everything would be okay, and then offered to listen if I needed to talk. I thanked him, and breakfast went on as usual."

"Do you think he killed Allen Weston?"

"I honestly don't know. The way he reassured me everything would be okay didn't strike me as strange at the time, but now ... I'm not sure if I actually suspect him or if I'm just in shock over the way he ran out of the shop that morning. It was so ... so unlike him."

"Why would you be in shock? He might not react that way often—okay, never—but you've gotta know by now that Mills has a thing for you."

Alma blushed. "Well, yeah, but I didn't know it was *that* big of a thing. He's normally so quiet, so predictable. I never expected him to react with such passion."

"What's the saying—'Still waters run deep'?"

"How deep is the real question," Stella mused aloud. "Deep enough to shoot Weston?"

With that, they heard the crunching of tires against the gravel and dirt camp road gradually drawing nearer.

"Good lord, it's Charlie," Alma announced as the Windsor County Sheriff car rolled into view. "Please don't mention what I've told you! If he isn't the killer and he finds out what I thought about him, it would hurt him so."

Having stopped his car behind the Buckleys' vehicle, Mills jumped out from behind the steering wheel and ran to the front porch of the cabin, leaving the driver's-side door open behind him. "Alma, thank goodness you're okay. I've been looking all over for you."

"I'm fine, Charlie. Why wouldn't I be?"

"Got a call that someone broke into your next-door neighbor's home."

"Oh my god! Bunny? Is she okay?"

Mills removed his hat and hung his head. "I'm sorry, Alma, but I'm afraid she's dead."

Chapter
15

ALMA, TOO DISTRAUGHT to drive, rode with Stella in the Smart car, while Nick in the pickup and Mills in the patrol car followed them to the trailer Alma shared with her brother. The scene that greeted them was like one from a television police drama. Emergency vehicles, their sirens muted, splashed the surrounding homes and trees with bright blue light while the inside of Bunny's doublewide, lamps glaring, cast an eerie glow into the inky Vermont darkness.

Haunted by her conversation with the dead woman, Stella delivered Alma to her brother and ensured that both were settled in before journeying next door, where she found Nick asking the sheriff to recount the details of Bunny's final moments.

"Come on," Nick urged. "You know we had nothing to do with this. Besides, it will be all over town by morning anyway."

"Nick's right. Why, just look at your deputy." She pointed to the young man in the uniform and wide-brimmed hat who was chatting up a pretty girl in the crowd that had gathered around the police cars.

Mills sighed. "All right ... the killer came in through the back bedroom window and shot the victim in the chest while she watched television. No struggle. Nothing missing. Hunting rifle again, so one bullet did the trick. Whoever did it came in, took care of business, and then took off."

"Who found her?" Stella inquired.

"Hank Reid. He and Bunny had a ... relationship. It being Saturday night and all, he called to see if she was free. When she didn't answer, he came by to check on her."

"Reid? And Bunny?"

"Jeez," Nick remarked. "Is there a warehouse of little blue pills in this town?"

"Huh?"

"Never mind my husband, Sheriff; he's being tested for Tourette's. We do have some things we need to discuss with you, though. Preferably where no one else can hear us."

Mills nodded and led the couple to his car. "This good enough? Or should we get in?"

Confident that no one was within earshot, Stella shook her head. "This should be fine."

"Okay, what is it you want to talk about?"

"We spoke to Alice about my conversation with Bunny last night." She launched headlong into the meeting at Vermont Valley Real Estate and Alice's word of warning.

"Those are exact words she used? 'Tell her to watch her back'?" he clarified when she had finished.

"Yes."

"And you figured you'd wait until someone else was dead to tell me all of this?"

Nick leapt to the defensive. "If memory serves me correctly, I told you about Bunny this morning at Alma's, but you dismissed her as an 'eccentric busybody.' And yes, those were the exact words you used."

"That was before Alice Broadman confessed to mortgage fraud and threatened another woman's life. Why you would keep something like that quiet is beyond me."

"Oh, and you haven't kept anything quiet, I suppose," Stella retaliated.

Sheriff Mills blanched. "What do you mean?"

"Alma told us about her relationship with Weston and how you ran out of the Sweet Shop the day before the murder. I'm sure neither of those details have made it into your case files. When did you plan on coming clean?" Stella hesitated before speaking again but decided to go for broke, if only to see the sheriff's reaction. "Or are you trying to cover the fact that *you* murdered Weston?"

"Now hold on a minute, there. I'll admit I had an axe to grind with Weston, but why would I want to kill some harmless gossip?"

"Because the night I met her at Perkins, Bunny mentioned your name as a suspect too."

"My name?"

"Bunny didn't know the extent of Alma and Weston's relationship, but she had noticed a certain chemistry between them. She suggested you'd noticed the same thing and did away with Weston out of jealousy."

"That's ridiculous!"

"Is it? Everyone in town knows you go to Alma's first thing every morning. It's obvious you have feelings for her. Even though I'm sure most people probably dismiss it as a silly crush, I'm certain it's more."

"All right," Mills yielded to Stella's reasoning. "What do you want me to say? That I care about Alma? Of course I do. That's why I was trying to protect her."

"By killing Weston?" Nick asked.

"No, not that the idea hadn't crossed my mind. I remember that morning at Alma's. Didn't want to pry, but I could see she'd been crying. Put up a brave front, she did, but she caved in the end. Didn't tell me details, just that she couldn't believe he had hurt her like that. That's what she kept saying over and over; couldn't even say his name. That's how upset she was.

"Again, I didn't want to push," Mills went on, "but I had to confirm my suspicions. See, Bunny was right. I had noticed Weston in the shop a few times, eyeing Alma up and down, so I had an idea he was the man in question, but I wanted—I needed—to hear it straight from Alma."

"Did she eventually tell you?"

"Yup. When she finally said his name, I felt my blood boil. Don't know if I've ever been that angry before. I flew out of the shop and drove directly to Weston's house."

"Was he there?"

"Yup, cocky son of a bitch came to the door in his bathrobe and slippers, looking like some backwoods Hugh Hefner. I was all ready to tear a strip off him, but he didn't give me a chance. Seems that, unknown to me, Weston had called the police before I left Alma's. He thought I was answering the call."

"Why did Weston call the police?" Stella asked.

"Spotted Maggie Lawson sneaking around his property."

"Looking for her treasure, no doubt," Nick inserted.

"She told you that story, huh?" Mills said.

"With gusto … and firepower."

"That's strange," Stella said. "Maggie told Nick and me that Weston had never called the police on her, but you're saying he had."

"I doubt she even knew about it. Though I still wanted to punch Weston in the face, I guess the cop in me kicked in. I looked around for Maggie but she weren't there. Disappeared into the trees, prolly. She's stealthy that way."

"Great," Nick exclaimed. "We're living next door to a trigger-happy ninja."

Stella rolled her eyes. "What happened when you couldn't find Maggie?"

"I went back to Weston, told him Maggie was gone, and then gave him a piece of my mind about Alma. You know that jackass acted like he didn't know what I was talking about? So I made it simple: if he went near Alma again, I'd shoot him. He got that message all right."

"You threatened to shoot him?"

"Now, don't give me that look, Mrs. Buckley. He was younger and in better shape." Mills placed his hands on his belly. "How else was I supposed to threaten him—with a lifetime of parking tickets?"

"No, I suppose not. Was that the end of your meeting?"

"Yup. Not much left to discuss after you threaten to shoot someone."

"Did you see Weston again before he died?"

"Nope. Gotta admit finding him in your well gave me quite a turn. Alma had been so upset 'bout what Weston had done to her that—and I'm not proud of it—I assumed she was the one who shot him. Then when she showed up later that day? Well … that's why I didn't tell you about meeting Weston and why I kept saying it was a hunting accident. I was trying to protect Alma."

"That's very noble of you, Sheriff, but doesn't it bother you that she might have killed a man?"

"It was starting to weigh on me a bit. That's why I'm so glad I found her with you tonight. That puts her in the clear."

"So it's a definite that the same person who killed Weston killed Bunny," Nick surmised.

"Not definite. We need the coroner's report. But pret' near certain."

"Um, not to rain on your parade, Sheriff," Stella interrupted, "but how long has Bunny been dead?"

"About two or three hours. Why?"

"We can't put Alma in the clear," Nick deduced.

"She was at our place when we got there. We never saw her arrive. She could have been there anywhere from six hours to six minutes."

Mills removed his hat and scratched his ginger hair. "I don't figure Alma would kill Bunny. She'd have no cause."

"No cause? If Bunny was as everyone says, she might have known the identity of Weston's killer. That gives all our suspects a reason to want her dead—including you, Sheriff. And Alma."

"Alma's gotta have an alibi."

"What about you? Do you have one?"

"I was in my car, driving home. Been there an hour or so when the scanner picked up the call."

"So neither you nor Alma have an alibi for Bunny's death."

"Look, I'll think of something. In the meantime, I'd appreciate it if you'd keep my threats against Weston under your hats."

"No problem," Nick reassured him. "You have our word."

"And, ummm ... the Weston and Alma affair too?"

"What? You mean you're willing to put your job on the line to protect Alma? Even if she's guilty?" Nick said disapprovingly. "I know you care about the woman, but if she killed someone in cold blood—"

"If she did, she had plenty good reason. Listen, I've seen lots of domestic violence situations. Women either accept it or they fight back—"

"Wait," Stella ordered. "Wait a minute. What are you talking about? Alma never said anything to us about Weston being abusive."

"She didn't? What did she tell you?"

"She told us she felt angry and hurt because Weston was seeing someone else."

"Is that why they ... ? When she said he hurt her, I—I thought she meant he got physical."

"Did she have bruises or cuts when you saw her?"

"No, but I didn't know if Weston, you know, forced himself on her."

"Sorry, Mills, I'm afraid she went gently into that good night," Nick joked.

"Oh," Mills said in a disappointed tone, but his mood quickly lightened. "That's great news."

"Yeah, I'm sure you're relieved. I know I'd be a mental case if someone ever laid a hand on Stella."

"There's that, sure. But if Weston didn't beat Alma, that means she's in the clear again."

"I'm not sure I follow your logic, Sheriff. If Weston cheated on Alma and then acted like a dirtbag during their breakup, she still has a motive."

"On paper, sure. But Alma wouldn't have killed Weston over another woman. If she was that type, her ex-husband would have been dead years ago. The only thing that would have pushed her over the edge was violence."

"It's not scientific, and it definitely wouldn't hold up in court."

"Don't matter. She's innocent and that's that."

Stella, meanwhile, was still incredulous. "So, let me get this straight: you've been sneaking around trying to protect Alma because you thought she shot Weston. Meanwhile, Alma ..." her voice trailed off.

"What?" Mills pressed. "What about Alma?"

"I can't. I promised I wouldn't tell anyone."

"If you don't tell me, I'll bring you in for questioning."

"You! After all you told me ...? You wouldn't dare!"

"Try me," Mills threatened.

Stella gave in. "Okay. Alma came over to the camp tonight to tell us she suspected you but didn't want to rat you out to your colleagues."

"Alma thought *I* was the murderer? Hmph ... imagine that. And she wanted to protect me?"

"She sure did. The last thing out of her mouth before you showed up was that she didn't want you to find out she suspected you. She was afraid you'd be hurt by it."

Mills's blue eyes sparkled. "She was concerned about hurting me?"

"Jeezus, it's like a twisted O. Henry story," Nick complained. "Next thing you know, you'll be buying each other combs and pocket watches. Although technically you're both still on the suspect list and none of this nonsense has provided either of you with an alibi, I, for one, think you're both too corny to have shot Weston. Which feels good, because I'm getting kinda attached to you crazy, lovesick kids."

"Thanks, Nick. Thing that doesn't make me feel good right now is taking Alice Broadman into custody. Woman has a husband and two young children."

"Do you have enough to arrest her?"

"Not for murder, but she did confess to mortgage fraud, and that's plenty serious these days. Could be in jail for ten years."

"Those poor people. It's not going to be a very happy weekend in the Broadman household," Stella sadly remarked.

"Nope. Say, why don't you folks head home? I'll be by in the morning with coffee, and maybe we can talk more about the case, if that's all right," Mills requested. "I'd like your input on some things."

"Sure," Nick acquiesced. "What do you think, honey?"

"Sounds good to me."

Mills nodded in agreement and headed back to the crime scene but not before pausing to shout back to Stella and Nick, "And hey, thanks. For everything."

Chapter

16

AFTER A GOOD night's sleep on the new air mattress, Nick and Stella sat on the front porch of the hunting camp awaiting the arrival of Sheriff Mills and, of equal importance, their morning coffee.

The sun had risen upon another unseasonably warm day, but whereas the previous day had been dry and clear, today's heat was already accompanied by an uncomfortably high level of humidity.

While Nick yawned, stretched, and surveyed the landscape, Stella, seated in one of the Adirondack chairs, continued her stitchery.

"I saw you get up and work on that last night," he commented.

"Yeah, I couldn't sleep. I was still wound up about Bunny's death and Alice's arrest."

"Me too, but when I finally crashed, I was out cold."

"Same here. The stitching helped."

"What are you making?"

"Oh, just a token for Raymond and Alma for letting us stay at the camp. I figured they could hang it on the wall here once we've gone."

"That would explain why you've included the word 'beer.'"

She smiled. "I'll do something a bit girlier for Alma. Then I'll frame them both, wrap them both up, and give them to her with a card."

"Yeah, a nice Hallmark that reads, 'Thanks for the free food and use of your shower. We're sorry your boyfriend was a jerk, that your neighbor was killed, and that we suspected you of being a homicidal maniac. PS: If you see a flashlight in your latrine, don't ask.'"

"Would I find that in with the sympathy cards or the thank you's?"

"Pretty sure it would be in the 'thinking of you' section. Might find it in with the cute kitten cards too, but I don't know—think a kitten might be over the top?"

"Maybe a little."

The sound of crunching gravel once again heralded the approach of Sheriff Mills, but unlike the previous evening, this morning found him behind the wheel of a blue Chevy pickup. He brought the truck to a halt beside the Smart car and stepped out of the cab.

"Wow," Nick remarked. "Look who's out of uniform. I almost didn't recognize you."

Mills, clad in faded jeans, sunglasses, a light green button-down short-sleeve shirt, and a pair of lace-up moccasins, grinned and lifted a tray of coffee from a diner in the next town from the seat beside him. "My civilian wear," he announced as he sat down on the porch.

"How'd it go with Alice?" Stella asked.

"Miserable. Tried to keep it low key, no cuffs and no sirens. But the kids woke up 'cause of her crying, and the neighbors saw me take her out. Feds are coming by tomorrow to take over the mortgage fraud charges."

Nick, dressed in a New York Knicks T-shirt and pair of cargo shorts, sat between the sheriff and Stella. "What about the murder case?"

"Alice and her husband took the kids to a corn maze and then supper at the bar and grill."

"So she has an alibi for Bunny's murder."

"Yup. She's the only one, though. Josh Middleton is still under house arrest for the truck incident, so he was at home watching a Netflix movie—alone—while his mother was at work. Maggie Lawson was out doing who knows what. Jake Brunelle was alone working in his shop. And Betsy Brunelle says she was in Rutland shopping."

"And we're back at square one," Stella noted as she put down her stitching and distributed the coffee cups.

"Yup, but it seems you've made some progress in your own investigation."

"I don't know about that. We may have unearthed some new things, but I still have more questions than answers."

"Well, throw them out there. Let's see what we can come up with."

"Okay." Stella took a sip of coffee and gathered her thoughts. "First off, why was Weston at our house? And don't say to work on our well, because we all know Weston never did the work himself."

"The only thing I can come up with," Nick offered, "is that he wanted to handle it himself in order to make a good impression."

"We spoke to Hank Reid, honey. Does it sound like Weston was the type to go out of the way for a customer?"

"No, it doesn't."

"So what other explanation could there be?"

"Might have been meeting someone there," Mills suggested with a shrug.

"That was my thought too. And a meeting would explain the last-minute change in schedule. However, why our house? We've seen his house, and it's—" Stella caught herself, but it was too late. Mills stopped drinking his coffee in mid-sip.

"When did you see Weston's house?"

"Um, we drove past just to check it out. You know, get a lay of the land," Nick explained.

Mills gave a doubtful frown.

"Anyway," Stella continued, "Weston lived on the top of a hill at the end of a long, private road. Alma met him there several times and no one ever saw them. If Weston needed privacy, he could have arranged a meeting at his place."

"Maybe Weston was at your house to meet with Maggie. She lives nearby."

"There are a few flaws with that theory. First, why not just meet Maggie at her house? She's told anyone who'll listen about the painting. If anyone saw Weston's truck in her driveway, they'd assume he was smoothing things over or asking her to leave him alone. Second, why did he need to meet with her at all? According to Maggie, she ran into Weston at the well office and the septic service shop last week. And by your account, Sheriff, she was at his house as recently as the day before his death. If there was something he needed to discuss with her, he could have done it then."

"But instead he called the police."

"Which raises another interesting question. Why did Weston suddenly feel the need to call the police? Maggie had been stalking him at work for weeks and he hadn't contacted the authorities."

"There's a big difference between stalking someone at their place of work and stalking them where they live," Nick said.

"Call me old fashioned, but stalking is creepy no matter where you do it. If the source of Weston's fear was Maggie herself, he would have gotten a restraining order weeks ago, but he didn't. Sooo..."

Nick and Mills leaned forward in anticipation.

"...what if what actually frightened Weston was that Maggie got too close to the painting or to something else he was trying to hide?"

"Great, now you're quoting Señora Psycho herself."

"Because, as crazy as the rest of her story might sound, that part makes sense. Why else would he have such a sudden change of heart?"

"Guess it might be worth looking into."

"Of course it is! Sheriff, do you think we could head over to Weston's house once we finish? I'd like to give it another look."

"Another look? I knew it! I *knew* you two broke in there."

"No, Stella broke in. I walked in the front door."

"*You* broke in?" The sheriff was incredulous. "What did you say you did in New York again?"

"I didn't say."

"It's classified," Nick replied. "Even I'm not allowed to know."

Stella rolled her eyes. "What does it matter if I broke in? I didn't take anything out. What *does* matter is that when I was there, I took a look at Weston's closet. It was filled with fancy suits and designer labels."

"So?" Mills challenged.

"So, what was Weston doing in a no-name flannel shirt and bargain-basement jeans?"

"Flannel shirt was brand new. I can only assume he bought it to work on your well."

"Not a man like Weston. Not a man who put creases in his khakis. If Weston needed work clothes, he would have bought them from Orvis or L. L. Bean or, if he were slumming it, from Woolrich. Instead, what he was wearing was strictly Walmart. It makes as much sense as him moving his truck into the woods."

"Maybe he was hiding?" Nick offered. "The next closest house belongs to Crazy Maggie. I wouldn't want that all up in my grill."

"Make up your minds! One minute you guys have Weston meeting Maggie; the next, he's hiding from her. If Weston wanted to hide from Maggie, he would sent one of his guys to our place to do the job. And he definitely wouldn't have driven past her place in a bright yellow truck with his name on it."

"Well, I'm stumped."

"Me too," Mills echoed. "Every time I think I have one question answered, another question pops up that my answer doesn't fit."

"I know," Stella agreed. "And we haven't even gotten to Bunny's death yet."

"What's so confusing about that? She was killed because she knew something about the murderer. Could be anyone, except for Alice. Oh, and Hank Reid."

"I noticed you didn't mention Reid earlier. Did he have an alibi?"

"Yep. Bunny's voice mail and Hank's phone records support his story."

"He lives just five minutes away from Bunny. Those phone calls mean nothing. He could have snuck over there between leaving messages."

"Yeah, but he and Bunny were …"

"Sleeping together?" Nick finished Mills's thought. "In my opinion, that makes him an even stronger suspect. Not only did the intimate nature of their relationship give Bunny access to Reid's house and personal belongings—which, for all we know, could have included some damning evidence—but Reid might have made an offhand comment or let something slip during … um … the heat of the moment."

"Eww," Stella said in disgust.

"I know. I think I just threw up in my mouth."

Mills wrinkled his nose. "All right, we'll add Reid back to the list of suspects."

"Good call, 'cause I think he's guilty. Guess what, honey, I'm riding the Cheney Train again!"

"The what?"

"Don't mind my husband. His good night's sleep has rendered him completely annoying. Anyway, now that we're all on the same page regarding suspects, there's just one nagging question left, and I'm afraid I might be the only one who can answer it—well, me and Perkins, that is."

"What question is that?"

"Nick, you remember how Bunny rushed out of the store that night?"

"Of course I do. I just about wiped out a shelf of Spam and corned beef hash trying to avoid her crashing into me."

"She was talking about something just before she ran off … it was you, Sheriff."

"Come on, now," Mills said sharply. "Haven't we already been through this?'

Stella waved a dismissive hand. "No, no, I don't mean it that way. She was talking about you but looking at something behind me. Something she saw or something she was talking about—or a combination of the two—struck a chord somehow. That's when she stopped what she was doing and hurried from the store. I'd like to try and re-create that scene if I could, so I can see exactly what she saw at the time."

"'Fraid you'll have to wait 'til tomorrah. Perkins is closed on Sundays."

"To most of us, perhaps. But I'm sure the Windsor County Sheriff might be able to finagle a special opening."

"Maybe." Mills downed the remainder of his cup and looked at Nick. "Is she always like this?"

Nick looked at the sheriff and replied tiredly, "You have no idea."

Chapter

17

Wedged into the cab of Sheriff Mills's pickup, the Buckleys and Mills made a brief stop at the Windsor County Sheriff's Department before making the drive uphill to Weston's house.

Upon reaching the gravel-lined driveway, the trio exited the vehicle and wended their way through the yellow tape to the front door. As he had done the day before, Nick pressed the thumbpiece of the brass front door handle. This time, however, the door would not budge. "It's locked!"

"'Course it's locked," Mills affirmed. "Don't want the whole town tramping through here."

"Yeah, but yesterday it was unlocked."

"You sure?"

"Positive."

"I don't see how that could be. I know I locked this place up Friday night."

"And I know I left it unlocked yesterday."

"It was unlocked, Sheriff. I even double-checked it," Stella joined in. "We wanted to make sure we left everything the way we found it."

"Then that would mean that someone either broke in ..."

"Or they had a key." Stella made no mention that only two of their suspects could have had such an object.

"Looks like we'd better go over this place with a fine-tooth comb. You see anything out of place, you tell me," the sheriff instructed as he took the house key from his pocket and opened the front door.

Stella and Nick stepped into the cool whiteness of the main foyer and made their way upstairs. Everything, from Weston's impressive collection of audio and visual equipment to his medicine cabinet full of restoratives, curatives, and elixirs, appeared to be intact and untouched. After a thorough exploration of the upstairs guest bedrooms produced the same result, Nick and Stella headed back downstairs to report to Mills.

On the way down, Stella whispered to Nick, "There are only three people who might have a key for this place. Weston's housekeeper, but no one's even mentioned her as a suspect, or if she even had one. Mills is the second, most likely Weston's copy."

"And Weston's girlfriend, i.e., Alma, would have had another. Maybe we should have kept an eye on Mills instead of letting him search alone?"

"It doesn't matter now. The killer was already here—whatever he or she was looking for is probably gone."

"But we haven't noticed anything missing."

"We'll check downstairs."

They walked into the kitchen, where they found Sheriff Mills rummaging through an island of cherry cupboards topped by a slab of dark gray granite. He stood up as they entered the room. "Find anything?"

"No," Nick replied. "Everything seems to be the same as we left it."

"Nothing moved, taken away, or added," Stella clarified. "At least, not that I noticed."

"Didn't see anything down here either. Guess we were wrong about someone having been back here."

"Someone *was* here, Mills," Nick rationalized. "And they came here for a reason. We might not be able to see what that reason is, but there has to be one."

Her suspicion of Mills renewed, Stella tried to throw him off course. "Probably just Crazy Maggie searching for her treasure."

Mills raised his eyebrows and pursed his lips together to imply that the Maggie scenario was a distinct possibility. "I'll go check the cellar, though, just in case."

As Mills disappeared through an interior door, Stella walked toward the front of the house.

Nick ran after her. "Where are you going? Shouldn't one of us go down there with him?"

"You go; I'll be right back. The ladies' room beckons."

As Nick returned to the kitchen, Stella retraced her steps into the foyer, pausing only to turn into the gray and stainless-steel powder room she had broken into less than twenty-four hours earlier. Closing the door behind her, she flipped on the light switch.

The sight revealed by the soft white glow of the vanity bulbs made Stella freeze in her tracks. "Nick! Sheriff Mills!"

She heard the sound of running footsteps as the two men scrambled out of the kitchen and through the foyer.

The door flew open.

"What is it?" Nick demanded. "Are you okay?"

Stella pointed at the vanity mirror.

Mills, gun drawn, was the first to enter. "What about the mirror?"

"Honey, if this has something to do with you needing a salon appointment—"

"No, it's the frame."

Mills put the safety on the gun and returned it to its holster. "What about the frame?"

"It's completely different than the one that was in here yesterday."

"Are you sure?" Nick asked.

"Positive. The frame in here was Baroque in style, carved wood with silver leaf. Looked to be quite old, too. I took note of it because it was so incongruous with the rest of the room. But this—" She examined the beveled edges and straight lines of the new frame. "This is—"

"Twenty-first century crap?"

"Basically. This crackled silver finish? A veneer, and not a very good one either. And the wood beneath it is so soft I can stick my fingernail in it. I'm going to guess it's pine. The mirror hasn't changed; it's attached separately to the wall. But the frame, which was installed as a finishing piece, is entirely different."

Nick stooped down and wiped some plasterboard dust from the floor with his finger. "This house might be new, but it's not that new. Besides, I think Mr. 'Crease in the Pants' Weston would have made sure that was cleaned up."

"Why would someone switch the frame on a bathroom mirror?" Mills pondered aloud.

"And why would they break in to do it?" Nick added.

"Treasure," Stella said in a near-whisper as she stared at the mirror frame.

"You mean that was—?"

"The painting? No, but that never was the real treasure, was it?"

Mills gave her a puzzled look. "I don't follow."

"I know you're not a regular television viewer, Sheriff, but have you ever heard of *Antiques Roadshow* on PBS?"

"Oh, you mean those fairs where people bring in junk and have it appraised? Yup, I know about those."

"Well, if you've ever seen someone bring in an old painting, then you'll know that very often the frame is worth far more than the item inside it."

"You mean …?"

"Art and frames aren't my area of expertise, mind you, but I believe the frame I saw in this room yesterday was an original sixteenth-century Rococo."

"How much would that be worth?"

"Given the size, condition, and age, a conservative estimate is anywhere from $15,000 and up. But, again, I'm not an expert."

"$15,000 for a frame?" Mills nearly choked.

"And I low-balled it." Stella pulled a cell phone from the rear pocket of her pants. "But I know a guy who can give us a more exact number."

"You can try and call him, but you're not getting through to anyone on that from here. Only two spots around here where those phones work—one is the area by your house, the other is the sheriff's department."

"Are you serious?" Nick exclaimed. "No wonder I couldn't get a signal outside Alice's."

Stella exhaled noisily. "Well, considering it's Sunday, I'd probably be waiting until tomorrow for a call back anyway."

"Prolly," Mills agreed. "But you don't have to wait to get into Perkins."

"I don't?"

"Nope. While I was at headquarters, I called Clyde and—how do you put it?—hooked you up."

"Sheriff," Nick said with a pat to Mills's back, "this could be the beginning of a beautiful friendship."

STANDING IN THE same spot Bunny had occupied two nights earlier, Stella stared silently at the far wall of the Perkins Family Store and tried to make a connection between the woman's strange reaction and the assortment of items gathered there.

The elderly clerk, whom Mills identified as Clyde Perkins, the store's owner, watched the scene with skepticism. "You had me come down here on a Sunday so that she could stare at a wall?"

"I told you it's police business," Sheriff Mills assured him.

Nick moved beside his wife. "Do you see anything?"

"I see lots of things, but nothing that makes sense." Her eyes darted from the rack of newspapers and magazines to the shelves of pain medications and first-aid items and then the vintage advertisements for Coca-Cola and Jarrett Rifles that hung above them.

"A picture will last longer," Clyde taunted.

"So will we if you're not quiet," Nick retorted.

"Come on, Clyde," Mills interjected. "Just let the lady do what she needs to do, and then you can go home."

"Don't listen to the old man, honey. Just take your time."

Heeding Nick's advice, Stella let her gaze linger on the magazine rack. Bearing periodicals of every sort, the pocket-style stand blocked the cover art of each issue, leaving only their titles visible. She read the name of each publication intently, but inwardly doubted that *Sports Illustrated*, *Good Housekeeping*, *Yankee*, or *Country Living* would prove of much value to the case.

Moving her focus to the first-aid and toiletries area, she realized that distance prohibited her from actually reading any of the labels. Only through the use of brand recognition was she able to determine the aspirin from the Tylenol and the Crest from the Aquafresh. Even then, she failed to see how adhesive bandages, Pepto Bismol, or Aqua Net hairspray might have incited Bunny to leave as quickly as she did.

Feeling defeated, she shifted her attention to the pair of vintage Coca-Cola advertisements that hung on the wall above. Bearing the traditional images of pretty, smiling young women drinking brown carbonated beverages, the first print featured a brunette in a white jacket and purple skirt. Seated at a chrome-trimmed lunch counter, the girl was turned slightly toward the viewer, the seat beside her conveniently empty as if to invite thirsty spectators into the scene. The second ad figured a Marilyn Monroe-esque blond in a white cowboy hat and yellow kerchief posed against a backdrop of mountains and horses. The vignette had been lassoed by a white rope that led to the Coca-Cola logo and the words Play Refreshed.

Juxtaposed against these post–World War II symbols of wholesome femininity hung a retro-style ad for Jarrett Rifles depicting two hunters—one in a suede Western shirt, a blue bandana, and jeans, the other in a green plaid shirt and tan pants—lying in the snow, attempting to shoot a buck in the distance.

Stella, deep in thought, frowned. *Was this what Bunny had seen? An ad for Jarrett Rifles?*

Nick noticed the change in Stella's facial expression. "What is it?"

"The only thing I can think of is that Bunny saw those ads."

Mills stepped forward. "Both she and Weston were killed with a hunting rifle. Don't know if—"

The three turned around to see Clyde hanging on their every word.

"I think we're done here," Stella announced. "Maybe we should go somewhere to talk—in private."

"Yeah, thanks, Clyde," Mills politely added.

"Welcome," the storeowner replied. "Did I hear you say you think the killer used a Jarrett?"

"Don't know. Why?"

"Hank Reid owns one. He was in here last week telling me how he was going to take his out bear hunting this weekend."

"Jarretts—they're custom jobs, aren't they?"

"Yup. Expensive too. Not likely to see many of them."

"Hmph." Mills led the way out of the store. "Well, thanks again, Clyde. See ya."

Clyde followed them outside and locked the store behind him before driving away in a dilapidated white van.

When he had gone, Nick gave a triumphant laugh. "Ha! I knew it was Reid!"

"Careful now," Mills warned. "We don't know that for sure. We'd need to match Reid's rifle to the bullet wounds."

"Yeah, but come on. Bunny looks up and sees her boyfriend's favorite hunting rifle advertised on the wall. She realizes he might have killed Weston and runs out of the store. Stel"—Nick always shortened his wife's name in moments of excitement—"do you remember what she was saying before she freaked out?"

"She was talking about how men will do anything to impress a—"

"A what?"

"She ran off before she finished the sentence. But considering she was talking about Sheriff Mills and Alma, I'm assuming she was going to say 'woman.'"

"See? Even that fits how Reid won over his wife by shooting her boyfriend."

"What it doesn't fit is why Weston was dressed the way he was and why he moved his truck into the woods."

"Easy. He was hiding from Reid. I'd hide from that old coot too if I were Weston."

"Why was Weston at our house in the first place?"

"To work on our well. Sometimes the obvious answer is the right one." Nick held his arms aloft and wiggled his knees back and forth.

"What is he doing?" Mills asked Stella.

"That's his victory dance," she said with a roll of her eyes.

"I solved it," Nick shouted. "I said it was Reid from the beginning, and I was right. Who's number one? Who's number one?"

"We won't know he did it until we check his rifle," Mills reminded him.

"Yeah, Nick, so keep it under your hat for now. Because if the ballistics don't match, you'll go from number one to looking like number two."

"Oh, they'll match, all right," Nick boasted as he climbed into Mills's pickup. "And do you know why?"

He pointed to his chest. "Because I'm number one," he silently mouthed.

Chapter
18

CUTTING HIS SUNDAY short in order to report his findings, Charlie Mills returned to the sheriff's department, dropping Stella and Nick back at the camp along the way.

Stella kicked off her black flats and sat cross-legged on the air mattress while she resumed her stitching.

"Since I've solved our crime, how about we take this evening off to celebrate? We can go outside and watch the sun set over the Green Mountains and then have an early dinner. I'll grill up those steaks Alma brought over, and there's still some wine and beer in the cooler. What do you think?" Nick sat beside his wife and wrapped a muscular arm around her shoulders.

"I think that a woman couldn't possibly have lifted that frame by herself."

With a heavy sigh, Nick flopped backward onto the bed. "What part of *the case is solved* and *let's take tonight off* confused you?"

"I'm sorry, I just can't get it out of my head. I know Mills thinks Maggie's behind the break-in at Weston's house, but I disagree. First of all, that frame is enormous and very heavy, I'm sure. It would take some strength and skill to get it off the wall, let alone carry it back home."

"Yeah, it's about the size of a plate-glass window, isn't it? And Maggie walks everywhere."

"Exactly. Can you imagine her bringing that through the woods? Secondly, Maggie referred to the painting as the treasure. I don't think she has any idea that the frame might be the valuable piece."

"You *think* it's the valuable piece, but you haven't confirmed that yet," Nick sat back up. "For all you know, Weston sold the painting and kept the frame as a souvenir. But it's all conjecture right now. As Mills said, we can't do anything about this until tomorrow."

"I know. I just can't stop thinking about it."

"Maybe you need a distraction," Nick reached over and grabbed the cross-stitch fabric from his wife's hands before reaching around her waist and kissing her.

"Keep that up and I might forget about the case altogether," she said with a seductive smile. "And I don't think I want to do that … yet."

"I can wear a Sherlock Holmes deerstalker hat if it will help remind you." He kissed her again, only to have her rear back.

"Wait! Oh my god, that's it!"

"What? What did I say? What did I do?"

"The deerstalker hat."

"Really? Jeez, had I known you found that such a turn-on, I'd have bought one years ago."

"No, no, no, I'm excited, but not excited that way."

"Shocking." Nick let his arms fall from around her waist.

"I'm excited because Weston's clothes were like your deerstalker hat."

"You do realize I'm not actually wearing one, don't you?"

"Yes, will you listen to me?" With a loud sigh, she stood up. "I'm saying that Weston's clothes weren't a disguise, they were a costume."

"Hallow—"

"I know, Nick, Halloween is three weeks away. It wasn't that type of costume. According to Alma, Bunny, and Mills, Weston was seeing a woman—someone other than Alma. Someone so desperate to remain unseen that she ducked down in the passenger seat of Weston's car."

"Right. What's your point? That everyone in this town is getting it on except for us? Because I'm already aware of that."

"Stop thinking of sex for a minute, will you? At least, stop thinking about sex between us—for the moment. Let's assume that Weston wants to meet up with this mystery woman. Where do they go? Between Alma's visits and Crazy Maggie lurking around, they can't go to Weston's house. It's too risky. And they've already been spotted traveling out of town together. Suddenly, the phone rings—it's Alice Broadman asking if Weston's company will service the old Colton house."

"That's our place."

"Yes, good, you're following. Weston knows the house is empty and somewhat secluded, so he offers to service the house"—"And his girlfriend," Nick inserted—"personally. He has his secretary schedule the appointment for that Wednesday and then proceeds to call his lover—"

"Wednesday? Our well was serviced on a Thursday."

"Weston's lover agrees to meet him at our house on *Wednesday* until, at the last minute, she can't break away. She calls Weston,

Weston has his secretary call Alice, and the rendezvous is rescheduled for the next day, which is Thursday."

"Okay. I'm with you so far, but what about the clothes?"

"Either at his girlfriend's request, or because he knows she likes the rugged type, Weston decides to play up the whole construction angle. He buys a plaid shirt and jeans—inexpensive, of course, because he never intends on wearing them in public or for very long and, well, they fit the part—and calls her when he arrives at the house."

"So that's who he was on the phone with when Alice arrived."

Stella nodded. "Knowing he'll have to actually work on the well after his assignation, Weston unloads the truck and then, so that no one will know he's there and possibly interrupt their afternoon delight, he moves the truck into the woods and walks back to the house, where his sweetie is waiting for him."

"On our air mattress. Good thing we got a new one."

"I hadn't even thought of that. Wow, that makes me glad we didn't…"

"Yeah, me too," Nick agreed. "So, who killed Weston? The girlfriend? That doesn't make sense."

Stella shook her head. "Despite Weston's best efforts, he was outsmarted. Whether he followed one of them there or overheard their phone conversation, the girlfriend's husband shows up later and shoots Weston in the chest."

"So all we need to do is find out who Weston was seeing, and the case is solved."

"I know who Weston was seeing. So did Bunny; that's why she was killed."

"Who was it?"

"Betsy Brunelle. Bunny figured it out that night at Perkins."

Nick knitted his eyebrows together. "How? From what?"

"The ads. Not just one, but the combination of them: a woman waiting for someone to join her, the cowgirl, and the hunters, one of whom looked very much like a cowboy, the other dressed in similar clothes to Weston."

"I still don't see the connection between the cowboys and Betsy."

"Didn't you notice her screensaver at the office? A slideshow of beefy cowboys—all with beards."

"Oh yeah. I thought it was weird for a married woman to have that on her computer, especially when her husband was right in the office. But given who she was married to …"

"Not only is Jake not very good looking, but he had been steadily losing business, whereas Weston was fairly wealthy. Remember, Betsy said her favorite pastime is shopping."

"And men. Don't forget the men. I know she didn't verbalize that, but she said it in other ways, and it substantiates your theory. My only question is, how would Bunny have seen that screensaver?"

Deep in thought, Stella lay back on the mattress. Several minutes elapsed before she spoke again. "Did Mills bring a newspaper with our coffee?"

"Yeah, it's on the front porch. Why?"

"I need to check something," she explained as she rose from the bed and ran out the front door with Nick in tow.

Retrieving the paper from its spot atop Alma's cooler, Stella perused a few lines and began to smile. "Here, look at that."

Nick took the publication from her hand and began to read out loud. "A sixty-two-year-old Windsor County woman was found dead in her home last night. Police report that Elizabeth 'Bunny'

Randall died as a result of two bullet wounds to the chest." He looked up. "Elizabeth Randall?"

"That's right. The office clerk the Brunelles hired and subsequently fired."

"Betsy said she fired Bunny because of some rotten habit. Did she mean snooping or gossiping?"

"Probably both. Betsy might not like being in the office alone all day, but if she were having an affair with Weston, having a 'nosebag' like Bunny around was even worse. By the time she was fired, I'm sure Bunny was aware that Betsy was seeing someone. Perhaps she even suspected it was Weston, but it took that night at Perkins for her to suspect the affair and Weston's death might be linked."

"But why not say something to you or the police? Why rush out of the store the way she did?"

"She and Betsy were friends, remember? Even though Betsy had fired Bunny, there still had to be some sense of loyalty. Bunny wouldn't want to reveal the affair to me or accuse Jake of murder without talking to her friend first."

"But Jake had an alibi for Weston's murder, didn't he?"

"How airtight is that alibi? Brunelle works alone; if the homeowners were out at the time of the installation, he could have left the property at any time. Likewise, when there's no traffic—and there wasn't any on Thursday morning—it only takes fifteen minutes to cut across town."

"But how would Brunelle have known Bunny was on to him?"

"I can only guess that Bunny left the store and hightailed it to the Brunelles' shop. Whether Jake overheard her conversation with Betsy or somehow ran into her and got suspicious is anyone's guess, but make no mistake: Bunny was murdered because she knew too much."

"And the frame?"

"Unrelated to the murder," she shrugged. "Either Maggie found a way to engineer the heist, or someone, like a maid or a housekeeper, realized what it was worth and took it."

"Someone who can recognize a Baroque silver-leaf picture frame?"

"Maybe there's another explanation, but I don't see how it could have anything to do with Weston's death."

"Me neither. So what do we do about Jake Brunelle? I know we have no solid evidence, but if the guy killed Bunny because she might turn him in, wouldn't he do the same thing to his wife if he thought she suspected him?"

"I was just thinking the same thing. We have to get Mills over there, and quick."

She pulled the cell phone from her back pocket and began to dial before noticing that she had no signal. "Grrr... outhouses, no cell phone service, no electricity, and a killer on the loose. Where the hell did we move to, Nick?"

"I don't know, but we'd better take the car and try to call Mills from the road before it's too late."

19

NICK DROVE AS fast as safely possible down Route 4 while Stella monitored her cell phone for the slightest hint of reception. "I thought Mills said we got service on this road," she complained.

"He meant the road outside our house, not the camp," he corrected as he stepped on the brakes. "We're stopping. Why are we stopping? What the hell is this?"

Ahead, a coach bus marked as being part of Happy Trail Bus Tours turned on its yellow flashers and crept along the two-way highway.

"Can you go around them?"

"I can't see what's coming, and it's a double-lined road."

A set of red lights came aglow as the bus ground to a halt in the middle of the traffic lane.

"What the—? Oh, come on! Why are you stopping?"

"Oh, Nick, we have to go around them somehow!"

"Don't worry, I'm on it." He swerved onto the shoulder of the road and began to accelerate in an attempt to overtake the bus from the right-hand side.

As the front bumper of the Smart car reached the back of the bus, the larger vehicle opened its doors, issuing forth an army of camera-toting senior citizens onto the dusty shoulder and outward into an adjacent field.

Nick slammed on the brakes.

"Leaf peepers," he and Stella said in unison.

"I can't believe it. The bus stopped in the middle of the road and is blocking traffic so that a bunch of tourists can take pictures of leaves."

"Let me handle this." Stella hopped out of the passenger-side door and fought her way through the crowd that had assembled alongside the bus.

"Hey," the passengers shouted as she walked in front of their camera lenses and bumped shoulders with everyone in her path.

"How rude," one woman could be heard remarking. "If this is what the locals are like, I'm glad we're staying in New Hampshire tonight."

"Believe me, lady, the state of Vermont heaves a collective sigh of relief as well," Stella replied as she stepped onto the bus through the open doors. There she found the driver, a heavyset man in his mid-thirties, sweating profusely and munching on a bag of Fritos.

"Sir? Sir, we need to get around you. Would you mind pulling onto the shoulder?"

"Ma'am, I'm not allowed to move this bus until every passenger is inside and safely seated."

"But this is urgent—a matter of life and death!"

"I'm sorry, ma'am, but those are the rules."

"How about flagging us past? Can you do that?"

The driver shook his head and kept on munching. "Those yellow flashers mean you can't pass."

"That's just for school buses. These are grown adults who should know better than to cross a busy roadway without looking."

"Ma'am, I'm sorry. If you have an issue, you'll have to take it up with the bus company—" he started, but Stella had already gotten off the bus and was standing in the lane of oncoming traffic.

"Come on, honey," she screamed at the top of her lungs. "It's clear!"

Nick revved the engine of the Smart car, causing the senior citizens in the nearby field to gape at him in horror. Shifting quickly into reverse and then into drive, he navigated around the bus and back into the right-hand lane before pulling to a complete halt at Stella's feet.

She opened the passenger-side door and jumped inside. "Don't think I've ever seen this car move so fast."

"Don't think I've ever heard you shout so loud when you weren't angry."

Nick pressed the accelerator, sending the vehicle speeding down the road at full throttle and reaching the Brunelles' shop five minutes later.

Stella and Nick stepped out of their respective sides of the car and quietly shut their doors. "I don't see the Brunelle Construction truck parked around here," Stella noted, "so maybe we're in luck and Jake's not home."

She led the way through the open front door of the building. Downstairs, the office and shop area were devoid of both light and people, but above them, they could hear the sound of country music and the creaking of floorboards.

Nick picked up the receiver of the front desk telephone and handed it to his wife. "First things first."

With a nod, Stella dialed the Windsor County Sheriff's Office and asked for Mills. Her call was directed to his desk, but alas, it was an automated voice mail system, and not the sheriff, that answered.

"Hi Sheriff Mills, it's Stella Buckley. We're at Brunelle Construction. Please come out here as soon as you can. We have reason to believe that Jake Brunelle is the killer." She hung up the phone and drew a deep breath.

"Maybe we should wait until he gets here?"

"And take the chance that Jake will come back in the meantime? No, we need to get to Betsy and warn her. I'll go upstairs and talk to her. You stay here and keep a watch for Jake. While you're watching, see if you can't find something around here that ties him to the murders."

Nick nodded in agreement and watched as Stella set off through the darkened shop. With one eye trained on the office window, he flipped through the stack of papers that were piled on Betsy's makeshift desk, only to encounter page after page of unpaid invoices.

The Brunelles' mounting debt provided Jake Brunelle with a strong motive for murdering Weston, but it still wasn't the concrete evidence they needed. With a deep breath, Nick returned the stack of papers to Betsy's desk and, reticent to step into the role of hacker, decided to search the office's single file cabinet before facing the challenge of navigating the company computer.

As the setting sun cast a purple hue on the unlit office, Nick moved toward the monolithic black cabinet at the back of the room. Picking his way through the gathering darkness of the old maintenance building, Nick failed to notice the thick extension cord that trailed across the office's dusty plywood floor. Within seconds, the toe of his sneaker was caught in the snakelike cable, sending him hurtling headlong toward the cabinet he had intended to quietly search.

Nick threw both arms outward, successfully catching himself by grabbing hold of a large cardboard box that rested against the adjacent wall. He immediately identified the mattress-sized parcel as the container for the Brunelle Construction sign.

He also recognized that, in his effort to brace his fall, he had mutilated an entire corner of the package, revealing, through the torn layers of corrugated paper, a faint glimmer of silver.

STELLA FOLLOWED THE sound of country music to a darkly stained plywood door. Not wishing to invade Betsy's privacy, she gave the door a quick rap. "Betsy? Hello?"

Despite the sounds of footsteps on the floor above, there was no reply.

Stella debated whether or not she should knock again. Determining that a double homicide was a suitable excuse for a breech in etiquette, and fearful of Jake's imminent return, she opened the door and climbed the narrow stairwell to the second floor.

At the top of the staircase, Stella was met with yet another door and, behind it, the smell of food emanating from a well-designed galley kitchen. Betsy, her back to the stairwell, was leaning over a small ceramic cooktop, singing along with the music of an unseen stereo. On the counter beside her rested a plate of flour riddled with meat drippings, a large butcher's knife, and a cutting board stacked with onion, celery, and carrots.

"Betsy," Stella called as she watched the dark-haired woman sprinkle something over the Dutch oven of browning meat. "Betsy?"

The woman whirled around in surprise, knocking the pan of meat off the burner and onto the linoleum-tiled floor.

"I'm sorry, Betsy. I didn't mean to—" Stella apologized until she noticed the yellow box of d-Con rodent poison in Betsy's right hand.

Before Stella could say another word, Betsy seized the butcher's knife from the cutting board and lunged forward.

"Nick!" Stella screamed as she stepped backward and held her arms up to defend herself. "Nick!"

Betsy took a stab at her chest, but Stella, her back against the closed stairway door, managed to roll her shoulders and torso out of the way. Reaching up, she clasped Betsy's arm tightly and, with one foot flat against the door for added leverage, used all her strength to try and push the knife-wielding woman away.

Betsy, however, was tenacious, and the two women, each straining to gain the upper hand, remained deadlocked for what seemed like an eternity. Stella, red faced and perspiring, felt the strength in her arms slowly start to drain and her grip on Betsy's arm gradually loosen.

As she struggled to think of her next move, an incredible force sent her tumbling forward onto her assailant. Betsy, unable to retain her balance, fell backward onto the linoleum floor, the impact of the hard surface knocking the knife from her grasp.

Stella, having landed at Betsy's feet with a loud grunt, quickly rose from her prone position and scrambled on her hands and knees for the knife. Betsy, meanwhile, rolled onto her stomach and extended an arm toward the weapon, her fingertips landing upon the black forged handle before Stella could get close enough to reach for it.

Stella caught her breath and braced herself for another attack. But just as Betsy raised the knife, a sneaker-clad foot came down upon her back, pinning her to the floor.

Panting and sweating, Stella looked up to see Nick standing over them. "Are you okay?"

She nodded and rose to her feet. "I think so."

Betsy, meanwhile, began to scream. "Get off of me! Let me go!"

Retrieving the knife as he did so, Nick bent down and pulled Betsy off the linoleum floor by her arm. "You try to kill my wife and you want me to let you go? I don't think so."

"I won't try to hurt you again, I promise," she sobbed. "I just don't want to go to jail."

"Maybe you should have thought of that before you tried to feed your husband rat poison," Stella rebuked.

"You don't understand. You don't know what it's like. Jake was going to talk."

"Talk about what?" Nick confronted her. "How you killed Weston? Or how you worked together to steal the frame?"

"She stole the frame?" Stella said in disbelief.

"It's downstairs in that big box that supposedly held their new sign. But it wasn't a sign, was it, Betsy? It was the replacement frame for Weston's mirror."

"You don't understand!"

"No? Why don't you explain it to us?" Stella offered.

"I loved Allen, I really did. He was better to me than any other man I'd ever known. He bought me presents and flowers and … he appreciated me. We had planned to run away together and leave this place … this hellhole where all I do is slave. But then … then I found out about *her*."

"Who?"

"Who do you think? Alma Deville. I went there one night to surprise Allen—Jake was working late—and her car was in his driveway."

"So you decided to take revenge."

"I wanted him dead for the way he treated me. For leading me to think—to think my life could ever get any better. I thought about doing it a few times, but I always lost the nerve. When he suggested we meet at your house, I saw my chance. It was perfect: empty, isolated. I even asked him to act out a little fantasy of mine, just so he didn't suspect anything was wrong."

Nick was incredulous. "You slept with him that day just so you could kill him?"

"Oh no, I would have slept with him anyway. It's a shame I had to kill him; the sex was incredible."

"Yeah, we've heard."

"And the frame? When did you come up with that idea?" Stella prompted.

"Around the same time. If I was going be stuck with my husband, I wasn't going to do it flat broke. Allen told me how much that thing was worth. Used to brag about how he stole it from right under Maggie Lawson's nose and how she'd never figure out it was the frame and not the painting that was valuable."

"But you couldn't steal it on your own. It was too heavy and cumbersome, so you recruited your husband to help. How'd you manage that?"

"I know Allen's housekeeper. I convinced Jake that she was the one who had told me about the frame. Jake hated Allen for taking away our business, so it wasn't hard to put him up to it."

"How did he get in? Did you give him your key?"

"No. Weston didn't give out keys," she replied matter-of-factly. "I climbed in the bathroom window."

Stella, crestfallen, looked at Nick.

"I'm still impressed, honey," he assured her. "Besides, you're cuter and, not to mention, saner."

Betsy frowned at him before continuing. "I unlocked the front door and left it open so that all he had to do was walk in, and then I rushed back here before anyone noticed I was gone. Jake could handle the frame, but I knew if I left the front-door thing to him, he'd goof it up."

"Guess what? Jake goofed it up anyway. He forgot to clean the dust from the bathroom floor after installing the new mirror."

Betsy's eyes grew wide. "Are you—? God, I'm sick of having to be the brains in this outfit."

"You may be the brains, but Bunny managed to outsmart you," Stella pointed out.

"Not really. She came here to warn me, same as you did. But I took care of her. Would have taken care of Jake too if you hadn't stuck your nose where it didn't belong."

A stocking-footed Jake Brunelle appeared in the doorway of the staircase. In his hands he cradled a hunting rifle. "Hey."

"Oh, Jake! Jake, thank god you're here," she cried in a burst of theatrics that rivaled that of any Academy Award winner. "These people, they've been holding me at knifepoint—"

"Save it. I heard it all. And I've had about all of you that I'm gonna take."

"Jake, please. You've got it all wrong. I love you!"

"Yeah, sure you do. That's why you were screwin' Weston all this time and why you were addin' rat poison to my venison stew, huh?"

Nick stepped forward. "Jake, don't do it. She's not worth it."

"You shut up! If you two hadn't been pokin' around in things that don't concern you, we wouldn't be here!"

With that, a shot rang out and both women screamed.

"Nick!"

"Jake! No!"

As Sheriff Mills and two uniformed officers climbed the staircase, Jake Brunelle dropped his rifle and grasped his bloody right arm in pain.

"Oh my god, Nick. I thought—" Stella rushed to her husband's side and threw her arms around his neck.

"I know. I thought I was a goner too."

As one officer handcuffed Betsy Brunelle, the other applied a tourniquet to Jake Brunelle's wounded arm.

"Sheriff Mills, I don't think I've ever been so happy to see the cops in my life," Nick joked.

Stella removed her arms from around Nick's neck and threw them around the sheriff's shoulders. "Thank you. Thank you for saving us."

His face a bright crimson, Mills cleared his throat and extricated himself from the young woman's embrace. "You're welcome. But next time, promise me you'll call 911 instead of using voice mail, you hear?"

As Betsy and Jake Brunelle were led downstairs, Jake shouted over his shoulder, "Goddamned flatlanders! Why don't you go home?"

Nick heaved a sigh of satisfaction and smiled. "Now that this is over, we will."

Chapter
20

Nick scooped Stella into his arms, carried her over the threshold of the Colton farmhouse, and deposited her in the living room to a round of applause.

"Congratulations," Mills told them.

"Years of happiness to both of you in your new home," Alma wished as she bestowed each of the Buckleys with a hug and a kiss on the cheek.

"Thanks," Nick smiled.

"Yes, thanks to both of you," Stella rejoined. "And as a token of our appreciation, I have a little something for each of you."

"You already treated us for dinner tonight," Alma argued.

"Don't worry, these are small, and I feel like celebrating—especially after learning that Alice's sentence has been lightened."

"Yup," Mills confirmed. "So long as she testifies against Weston's partner in Jersey, the most she'll see is house arrest. Things'll be tight with only Tim's income, but at least they'll be together."

Stella presented Mills and Alma with three gift-wrapped parcels. "Alma, there's one in there for you—inspired by those coupons you gave us the first day we got here—and another you can share with Raymond. And Mills, that one in the blue paper is for you."

Mills opened his and smiled. "*Never, Ever Question the Sheriff's Judgment*," he read aloud and held the frame aloft. "I'm going to hang that up at work."

Alma opened the package for her and Raymond: "*Johnson-Deville Hunting Camp: We Have the Deer, You Bring the Beer.*" When the laughter subsided, she opened the second, which read *Bitch in Kitchen*. "Ain't that the truth! Stella, sweetie, did you make these?"

"Yes, I designed them too. Why?"

"Because I love them. They're adorable and sassy—just like me. And so clever. You know, I never did get to ask, but what *did* you do back in New York?"

"It's classified," Mills and Nick said in unison.

"Oh," Alma said with a confused look on her face. "Well, if you're not too busy fighting crime, I'd love to sell these in the shop. My customers will flip over them."

"Sure," Stella shrugged. "Seeing as classified jobs are somewhat scarce at the moment, I'd love to."

"Wonderful. We can discuss it more at the shop next time you're in. But for now, I'm heading home."

"So soon?"

"Yep. Need an early start tomorrah. Jelly doughnuts don't make themselves." Alma looked at Mills. "Speaking of jelly doughnuts, would you care to escort a lady to her car, Sheriff?"

Mills looked up from his cross-stitch piece in astonishment. "I—I'd love to, Miss Deville."

Nick and Stella watched from the doorway of their new home as Alma and Mills, in their pickups, drove down the pothole-laden driveway. When they were nearly out of view, Stella closed the door with a sigh and said, "Thank goodness life is back to normal."

"Yup."

"The weather is cool again."

"Yup."

"We're in our new home."

"Yup."

"The Brunelles are behind bars."

"Yup."

"And we can finally relax."

"Yup."

Stella put her arms around his shoulders. "What's with the Vermont accent?"

"Oh, just trying to blend," Nick explained and slid his hand around Stella's waist. "Especially since we have to go back to the hunting camp tonight."

Stella's arms dropped to her sides. "The hunting camp? Why?"

"Because our new bed won't be here until tomorrow."

"So?"

He pointed to the air mattress that had been used by Allen Weston and Betsy Brunelle. "So, guess what we forgot to replace."

Stella looked at the spot indicated. "Eww."

"Yup."

"Well, let's go get the mattress," she sighed. "But this time, can we deflate it *before* we move it?"

Nick smiled and opened the front door. "Yup."

The End